The
Straightened Road

The Straightened Road

A Novel

Warren Moss

This is a work of fiction. While the novel is based in part on real incidents in the Ozarks, the characters, names, events, and dialogue are products of the author's imagination or are used fictitiously. Any resemblance to actual persons, living or dead, or to actual events beyond those broadly referenced, is coincidental.

Copyright © 2026 Warren Moss

All rights reserved. No part of this publication may be reproduced, distributed, or transmitted in any form or by any means, including photocopying, recording, or other electronic or mechanical methods, without the prior written permission of the copyright holder, except in the case of brief quotations embodied in critical reviews and certain other noncommercial uses permitted by copyright law.

ISBNs:
- Paperback: 978-8-994605-0-0
- Hardcover: 978-8-9946405-1-7

First Edition

Printed in the United States of America
10 9 8 7 6 5 4 3 2 1

For my mother, who held the world steady—
my father, who taught me the weight of quiet—
my brothers, and our time together—
and God, for the lake.

PART ONE

CH 01

The Call

THE CALL CAME while Scott was loading the car late Friday afternoon, in a driveway outside Chicago.

His mother didn't say hello. She said, "I need you down here."

He set the cooler on the driveway and kept one hand on the handle. Plastic sweated under his palm.

"What happened?"

"The septic," she said. "They flagged it. There's an inspection. If we miss it, we're in trouble. I can't do this by myself."

He'd been coming anyway. Now it had a deadline.

He waited for the rest of it. The part she wouldn't say first.

He pictured Brian in North Carolina, already deciding what to do with his hands, already making a list. Fifteen hours on the road if you didn't stop long. The kids couldn't just appear. Someone had to bring them.

"Is Dad—" he started.

"He's here," his mother said. "He's fine. He just... forgets. Some things."

He looked across the street at the neighbor's sprinkler ticking back and forth, the steady arc of water landing in the same two places, again and again, like it was practicing.

"When is it?" he asked.

"Tuesday. They're coming. We have to dig and fix what we can fix before that." Her voice stayed practical. That was how she carried fear. She put it in lists. "Can you leave today?"

"I already talked to Brian," his mother added. "He says he's on his way—from North Carolina. I can't get Matt. He's out west."

"I'll be there," he said.

"I told Julie to bring the kids," his mother added. "Drive them if she can. Fly if she has to." She paused, just long enough for him to hear his father in the background, asking a question she didn't answer. "Just come."

Scott ended the call and stared at his cooler like it had become a decision.

His phone screen filled with the rest of his life—calendar blocks, a voicemail badge, a message thread from his boss. He opened it and typed, I'm out through Tuesday. Family emergency. Back Wednesday.

He hovered over send long enough to feel childish.

Then he hit it.

Scott didn't mention to his mother the way his own gut clenched when she said forgets.

Scott tried Matt next.

Matt didn't answer. No voicemail greeting. Just ringing until it stopped.

Scott texted anyway: Mom called. Septic. Inspection Tuesday. You coming?

The message sat there without a reply.

Scott drove until the lights on the interstate blurred and his shoulders went numb. He pulled into a rest area and slept sitting up for a few hours, then got back on the road before sunrise.

By Saturday afternoon, Scott had driven far enough southwest that the roads narrowed and the trees moved closer.

Brian's truck was already in the gravel lot near the cabin when Scott pulled in. It sat angled wrong, too close to the edge, as if the driver had been in a hurry to stop and hadn't corrected afterward. The engine was off, but the hood still gave off heat.

Matt's car wasn't there.

The air smelled like hot limestone and damp ground. Somewhere down the shore, someone had a burn pile going—thin smoke, leaves and paper, the smell hanging low under the trees. A boat motor started somewhere across the cove and then cut out, the sound hanging a moment before it disappeared.

His father came out onto the porch in a clean T-shirt, holding a cup like it might spill if he didn't pay attention. He looked thinner than the last time. His shoulders were still broad, but the shape of him had softened, the way wood softened after too many wet seasons.

"You made good time," his father said.

"Yeah," he said. "Traffic wasn't bad."

His father nodded, satisfied, and stepped down carefully, one hand on the railing. He stopped at the bottom as if he'd forgotten what came next.

His mother came out behind him, moving with purpose, dish towel in her hand even though there was nothing to dry. She touched his father's elbow lightly and guided him toward the car without looking like she was guiding him.

Then she came to him and wrapped her arms around him, dish towel and all. It was quick and tight, like she could do it and still keep moving. Her cheek was warm against his shoulder.

"You came," she said into his shirt.

His father looked at him and smiled, as if he'd just found the right face in a room. "Well," he said. "There you are."

Brian came out then, finally, wiping his hands on his jeans. He hesitated at the top step like he was deciding whether to be a brother or a man with a list.

He came down and pulled him into a quick one-arm hug, hard enough to count. His hand hit Scott's back once and then let go.

He looked past him at the car and then at the water, as if checking weather.

"Hey," Brian said.

"Hey," he answered.

They stood there with the weight of years between them and the ordinary tasks of the next few days waiting to be named: digging, repairs, paperwork, something with a deadline.

His mother clapped her hands softly, like she was calling a room to order. "We'll unload you," she said. "Then I'll show you what the inspector said."

They carried bags inside. The cabin smelled like pine and old cooking grease and the sweet stale odor of lake water that lived in wood no matter how long you left it.

His father stood in the kitchen doorway, watching them move through the room. "You remember where the extra—" he began.

"Tools are in the shed," Brian said, quick. Too quick.

His father nodded like that had been what he'd meant. He lifted his cup and drank, then made a face at the temperature, as if the coffee had betrayed him.

He stepped out back toward the dock while the others talked. The boards were sun-bleached and worn smooth at the edges. The lake was lower than he remembered. A line of rock that used to stay hidden lay exposed along the shore. Old timbers, black with algae, stuck up at angles near the waterline like bones that hadn't been meant to show.

From somewhere out on the water came a high, whining sound. A wave runner cut across the channel, too fast for the space, rider standing up like it was a game. It threw a wake that slapped the dock and made the boards shift under his feet.

His father stood at the top of the steps, one hand on the railing. He stared at the water the way he always had, measuring it. Then he looked back toward the cabin and frowned, as if he couldn't remember what room he'd left something in.

"Dad," he said.

His father turned. "Yeah?"

He didn't ask the question then. Not on the dock with the lake shifting under them.

* * *

By late afternoon, headlights turned into the drive and crunched over gravel.

Julie—Brian's wife—climbed out slow, shoulders tight, and stood for a second like her body was still moving down the interstate. Jake came around the passenger side with a backpack and a look that said he wasn't impressed by the distance. Emily got out with her phone in her hand, eyes flicking up and away from the screen as if she didn't want anyone to think she'd been looking at it the whole time.

His mother crossed the yard and hugged her quick and tight. The two women said a few practical things in low voices—where to put bags, what time it was, what the plan was—and then stopped, like there wasn't room for anything else yet.

His father brightened when he saw the kids. That part was intact. It made him feel relieved and sick at once.

His father hugged Jake too tightly, then laughed and loosened his arms. "Look at you. You're getting big." He turned to Emily. "And you—"

He stopped, searching for the name.

His mother stepped in without making it a rescue. "Come on," she said to Emily. "Show him what you brought."

Emily held up her phone, obedient. "I have a video," she said.

His father leaned in, squinting. "A video," he repeated, tasting the word like it belonged to someone else's mouth.

After supper, his mother carried a coffee can of kindling down to the seawall.

There were old stones there in a rough circle—years of small fires, bottle caps half-buried in dirt, ash worked into the ground. Brian brought a couple pieces of split wood from the pile by the shed, oak that snapped when it caught. His father came down slow and sat in a folding chair, cup still in his hand, eyes on the water as if it could tell him what day it was.

Jake and Emily found sticks and made the fire their job. Jake poked at the edges and tried to make the flames stand up taller. Emily filmed a few seconds of it, then stopped and stared at the screen as if deciding whether it was worth keeping.

Scott sat on the seawall with his elbows on his knees and watched the fire turn wood into something lighter.

His phone stayed dark.

If Matt came, it would be tomorrow, rolling in late like he was doing everyone a favor.

He asked because he needed a place his father could still reach. A first thing. A shared thing. The only kind of proof that mattered.

"Dad," he said again, closer now. "You remember the old HH bluff road?"

His father's face stayed open, polite. "The what?"

He felt his own mouth go dry. He nodded once, like he'd only been asking casually. "Nothing."

The smoke shifted with the wind. It stung his eyes.

And underneath it, sharp and specific, he could smell hot brakes.

The engine sound came through the floor first.

It sat in their bones the way bass did on the radio—low and constant, vibrating the fiberglass and the thin metal parts that weren't meant to carry anything but speed.

Scott was wedged behind the two front seats with Brian and Matt, knees up, shoulders pressed together, the three of them packed into the carpeted space like duffel bags. The vinyl backs of the bucket seats were warm and slick. When Rick shifted, the car lurched and the boys slid as one, skin on skin, then caught themselves on the center tunnel.

"Quit it," Brian said, not because anyone had done anything yet, but because he liked setting the rules.

Matt's hair stuck to his forehead. He pushed it back and left a stripe of sweat. "I'm not doing anything."

Scott didn't answer. He watched the speedometer through the gap between Rick's shoulder and the steering wheel. The numbers moved in a way that made his stomach feel too light.

Linda sat in the passenger seat with a paper sack at her feet and a folded map on her lap that kept trying to unfold itself. Every few miles she refolded it, tighter, as if she could make the road smaller by forcing the creases.

The windows were down. Wind roared in and snapped at the edges of the map. The smell inside the car was hot vinyl and gasoline and the sharp clean bite of Linda's sunscreen.

On the radio, a man's voice came in and out under a country song. Glen Campbell singing "Rhinestone Cowboy." The signal thinned whenever they dipped into low places. Rick kept one hand on the wheel and one on the shifter, forearm tanned, wrist loose, driving like it was something he did for fun even when his sons were stacked behind him like cargo.

They had started in St. Louis early, before the day got fully hot. Now the sun sat higher and the car felt smaller by the minute.

Matt pressed his cheek to the window for a second and then jerked back. "It's burning."

"Stop touching things," Brian said.

Linda twisted in her seat just enough to look over her shoulder. Her eyes landed on all three of them at once, taking inventory. "Nobody hits. Nobody bites. You hear me?"

Brian nodded like he'd been the one keeping order.

Matt nodded too, quick.

Scott nodded because nodding was the easiest way to keep the peace moving forward.

Rick didn't look back. "We'll be there soon," he said, and Scott could tell it wasn't a promise. It was a way to end the conversation.

The car ran steady for a while. The road was wide enough that Rick stayed relaxed, drifting a little within the lane. The Stingray's hood stretched out in front of them, long and sloped, like it was already leaning into whatever came next.

Scott kept watching the speedometer. He didn't know much about cars, but he knew what the numbers meant. He knew what it felt like when the road began to tighten and Rick did not slow down enough to match it.

At a gas station in Foristell, just off I-70, Rick pulled in fast and braked late. The boys' bodies swung forward and then slammed back. Matt's elbow hit Scott's ribs and Scott bit the inside of his cheek hard enough to taste blood.

"Jesus," Linda said, not as a prayer. She reached out and put her palm on the dashboard as if the car might keep moving without permission.

Rick killed the engine and the sudden quiet made Scott's ears ring. In the silence, cicadas screamed from the trees beyond the pumps.

"Out," Linda said. "All of you. Stretch."

The three boys spilled out through the passenger door in an awkward sequence—Brian first because Brian always went first, then Scott, then Matt, who had to be pulled by the wrist because there wasn't room for him to stand up cleanly.

Standing upright felt wrong for a second. Scott's legs tingled. The sun hit the top of his head and made him squint hard.

Rick leaned into the driver's side window and paid the attendant without looking at his sons. His posture stayed loose. The car's paint gleamed. People looked at it even as they pretended not to.

Matt hovered near the rear quarter panel, running his fingers along the curve of the body like he couldn't help it.

"Don't," Brian said, but he didn't pull Matt away.

Linda unwrapped sandwiches and handed them out as if feeding them could keep them from fighting. The wax paper stuck to the bread in places.

"No crumbs in the car," she said.

Rick smiled once, quick. "This car doesn't have a back seat. Where do you think crumbs go?"

Brian laughed like it was a joke. Scott didn't laugh. Matt didn't either.

They got back in. The vinyl backrests were hotter now. Scott pressed his shoulder against Brian's and felt the sweat through the thin fabric of their shirts.

After they left the interstate, the road changed. The lanes narrowed. The shoulders turned to gravel. Trees moved closer to the pavement, and shade came and went in quick strips across the windshield.

Linda stopped reading the map and held it flat against her thigh.

Rick turned the radio down without being asked.

Scott watched the speedometer again. When the road started to bend and dip, the numbers didn't drop enough. His knees braced without him meaning them to, and Brian's arm flashed out once to catch himself, then fell back like it hadn't been anything.

Matt made a sound between a laugh and a gasp the first time the car swung wide and then snapped back. He liked the feeling of being pulled.

"Be quiet," Brian said, but his voice was strained.

They passed signs that said LAKE OF THE OZARKS in big letters, as if the place needed announcing. They passed billboards for restaurants and resorts and bait shops. Scott tried to imagine the lake from the signs—blue water, clean boats, smiling families—and couldn't make it match the heat and the cramped dark space behind the seats.

The sun dropped lower as they came into town. The road fell into tight curves and brake lights, then rose onto Bagnell Dam.

As they rolled onto the dam, cliffs and trees fell away and the lake opened up, wide and darkening, the main channel laid out beside them like a road made of water. Scott pressed his face closer to the glass and looked across at the boats moving, small white wakes trailing behind them, lights starting to show one by one as the day went orange.

He felt the height in his stomach. He felt the drop on both sides even without looking for it.

Rick wanted to speed up, but the traffic was heavy.

On the other side, the Strip hit them all at once.

Neon signs already flickered on though the sun hadn't fully left. Restaurants and marinas and cheap shops stacked close to the road, windows full of lake things and summer things. People crossed between parked cars in swimsuits and sandals, skin still wet, hair slicked back. The smell blew in through the open windows—fried food, gasoline, sunscreen, sweet smoke from somewhere cooking meat.

The Stingray idled with the rest of the traffic, then surged and stopped and surged again, Rick's foot impatient. Scott could feel the engine's heat through the carpet and the way Brian's knee kept bumping his because there wasn't anywhere else for it to go.

Then Rick signaled right and took HH into "The Bend"—the winding road over the bluffs—and Linda's hand went back to the dashboard again. She didn't say anything. She didn't have to.

The road tightened like a belt. Trees opened in places and the land fell away, and Scott caught a flash of water down below through the gaps—dull green-brown, too far to trust.

Rick drove like he knew the road, and that was supposed to make it safe.

Scott watched the speedometer and felt his insides clench the way they did on playground swings at the top of the arc. The car creaked over bumps, fiberglass shifting with its own small complaints.

Matt leaned forward until his forehead nearly touched the back of Linda's seat. "I can see it," he said.

"Sit back," Linda said, sharper now.

Matt sat back, sulking, knees pressing into Scott's thigh.

Scott didn't move away. There wasn't room.

The curves came faster. Gravel whispered under the tires at the edges. Rick's hands stayed calm on the wheel. Scott tried to read his father's face in the rearview mirror and saw only eyes, focused and bright.

For a moment, Scott thought about saying something—about asking Rick to slow down. The thought rose in his throat and then fell back down. He imagined the way Rick's jaw would set. The way Brian would look at him like he'd betrayed them.

He kept watching the speedometer instead.

Then the road dropped and leveled, and the trees thickened again, and the air changed—dampness in it, the faint smell of water even with the windows down.

Rick turned the radio up a notch, not loud, just enough to fill the silence.

Linda let her hand fall from the dashboard. She exhaled and looked out the windshield like she could see the cabin already.

Scott sat back against the carpeted wall behind him and felt the vibration of the engine settle into his spine again. His legs were numb from being folded.

Brian said nothing for a long time.

Matt said nothing too, which told Scott more than anything Matt could have said.

When Rick finally turned into the gravel drive, the tires crunched loud and familiar. The car bounced once, twice. The lake opened up beyond the trees like a held breath letting go.

Rick eased the Stingray to a stop.

The engine cut off.

In the sudden quiet, Scott could hear water somewhere—small slaps against wood, steady and indifferent.

CH 02

The Cabin

MATT ARRIVED near the end of the afternoon, the sun already shifting toward the trees.

The rental car sat wrong in the gravel—too clean, too new, plates from a different state. Owen climbed out of the back seat with headphones still on and looked around like he'd been dropped in someone else's memory.

Matt stood for a second with the car door open and listened.

He could hear the lake before he could see it—distant engines on the channel, a faint slap of water somewhere below the bluff, cicadas filling the spaces.

Brian's truck was already there, parked at an angle like he'd stopped in a hurry. Scott's car sat beside it, dustier, packed with road things—empty coffee cup, a folded map, a sweatshirt thrown across the back seat.

Linda stepped onto the porch when she saw them. She didn't wave. She just stood there with one hand on the screen door frame, eyes fixed, as if watching was the only way to keep the moment from slipping.

Matt shut the car door and walked toward the cabin, suitcase wheels bumping over gravel.

Brian met him halfway down the path.

For a second, neither of them moved like they knew what to do with their hands.

Then Brian stepped in and hugged him, quick and hard. One arm around Matt's shoulders, the other across his back, a squeeze that was more force than comfort.

Matt hugged back and felt his own ribs tighten, surprised by how much it landed.

Brian pulled away first and looked at him like he was checking for injuries. "You make it," he said.

Matt nodded. "Flight was a mess," he said, and the sentence was a placeholder for everything else he didn't want to say yet.

Scott came down the steps next, moving slower, watching.

Matt and Scott hugged too. Less hard. Longer. A back pat that almost turned into a joke and didn't.

Scott said, "Good to see you," and it sounded like a decision.

Matt nodded again. "Yeah," he said.

Behind them, Owen hovered with his backpack on one shoulder, eyes on the dock, the trees, the cabin, taking in what was new and what felt old in other people's faces.

Brian turned toward him. "Hey," he said, voice gentler. "You Owen?"

Owen pulled one earbud out. "Yeah," he said.

Brian nodded once like that was enough. "I'm Brian," he said, then pointed at Scott. "That's Scott. You remember?"

Owen glanced at Scott and gave a small nod. He didn't move closer.

Matt said, "He's been in airports all day," as if explaining the distance.

Scott nodded. "Come on," he said, and stepped aside to let them pass.

Linda came down from the porch and hugged Matt without hesitation.

Her arms around him felt different than when she'd hugged him as a boy—lighter now, as if she was careful of her own body, careful of his. Her cheek pressed briefly against his shoulder. He smelled her shampoo and smoke and something clean.

"Thank you," she said into his shirt, and the words were too plain to be casual.

Matt's breath caught. He patted her back once and then held on a beat longer than he meant to.

When she let go, her eyes were wet and then not. She looked past him toward Owen. "Hi, honey," she said, and smiled like she could choose it.

Owen nodded and said, "Hi," polite, cautious.

From inside the cabin, Rick's voice rose and fell, talking to someone on the phone—directions, maybe, or a schedule. Then the phone clicked down and his footsteps came to the screen door.

Rick stepped out onto the porch with his hat on. He stopped when he saw Matt.

For a second, Matt thought Rick was going to treat him like a neighbor—handshake, a nod, a distance that said adulthood.

Instead, Rick came down the steps and pulled Matt into an awkward hug, too high, his chin bumping Matt's shoulder.

Rick held on, then let go abruptly like he'd remembered what men were supposed to do.

"Look at you," Rick said, and his voice wobbled on the sentence.

Matt smiled because it was easier than any other face. "Hey, Dad," he said.

Rick nodded hard. "You made it," he said, as if Matt had fought his way here.

Matt said, "Yeah."

Rick's eyes flicked to Owen. "And who's this," he asked, and Matt felt the question hit like a small scrape.

Linda said, gently, "That's Owen," and her hand touched Rick's arm, a quiet reminder.

Rick blinked, then smiled too big. "Owen," he repeated. "Right. Come here."

Owen stepped forward because he was a good kid. Rick patted his shoulder like he was checking the firmness of it.

"Strong," Rick said, approving.

Owen nodded, uncertain what he was supposed to do with the approval.

Brian picked up Matt's suitcase without asking and carried it inside as if moving weight was easier than standing in feelings.

Matt followed them through the screen door.

Matt set his bag down inside the cabin and stopped.

Heat lived in the boards, and the air smelled of damp wood and old towels no matter how long you left the place shut.

Owen came in behind him with his phone in his hand, wrinkled his nose, and kept walking. Matt stepped to the screen door and looked down at the dock where the water stayed dark under the boards.

Matt went down the steps anyway.

The dock boards were warm under his bare feet. The water underneath looked close and far at the same time, shadowed where the foam floats held it.

Owen sat on the steps with his phone in his hand, screen bright against his face. He wasn't doing anything wrong. He was just sitting there like the dock was a chair and the lake was background.

Matt leaned over the edge and looked down.

Owen glanced up. "What are you doing?"

Matt straightened. "Nothing," he said, and heard how much like a kid it sounded.

Owen went back to his screen.

From the porch, Linda called someone's name. From inside, a drawer slid open and shut. The cabin was making its noises like it had never stopped.

Matt watched his son's bare feet on the step boards, toes hanging over the edge where the water started.

He wanted to tell him a rule. He wanted to tell him a reason. He didn't know which one would land.

Owen swung his feet once, careless.

Matt said, "Stay on the steps."

Owen looked up, already annoyed. "Why?"

Matt stared out at the cove mouth where the channel opened wider, bright and busy even from here. He chose the smallest true sentence he could.

"Because if you slip in right there," he said, nodding at the shadow under the dock, "no one can see you fast enough."

Owen's face changed. Not fear. Attention.

He pulled his feet back onto the boards without another word and sat still, phone in his lap, screen still glowing.

Matt stayed where he was and listened to the dock tap once under his heel, then again.

That summer, the cabin smelled like old wood and heat.

Not fresh pine. Not campfire. Something older than that—sun baked into boards, damp that never left, a sweet sour smell that clung to towels even after they dried on the line.

His father parked close enough that the front bumper nearly touched the grass. Gravel popped under the tires and then settled. The engine clicked as it cooled.

"Everybody out," his father said, already opening the trunk.

Matt slid out last because he'd been stuck in the middle of the back seat, and someone's elbow was always in his ribs. His feet hit gravel and he felt the little stones shift and bite through the soles of his sneakers.

Cicadas pulsed in the trees. The sound filled the whole cove like it was coming from inside his head.

His mother stepped around the car and looked at the cabin the way she always did at first—counting windows, checking the roofline, finding where the shadows lay. Then she smiled and pretended she wasn't doing that.

"Go," she told them. "Touch it if you want. Just don't run on the dock."

He didn't run. He walked fast. That was different.

The porch boards were warm under his hand when he grabbed the railing. The screen door had a torn corner where the mesh sagged. It slapped shut behind Brian when he pushed through without holding it.

Inside, his father moved like he knew where everything already was. He didn't look around. He went straight to the kitchen and opened cabinets. He pulled down a pan and set it on the stove. He checked the fridge, then shut it hard enough that bottles inside clinked.

"Where's the matches?" his mother asked.

His father didn't answer right away. He opened a drawer, then another. Then he nodded once like he'd found what he expected and held up a book of matches from a bar in town.

"Same place," he said.

Matt didn't know what that meant. Same as when? Last year? Before he was born? The cabin held time like that.

Outside, the dock creaked as his brothers stepped onto it.

He followed them down the worn steps, one hand on the rail. The wood was rough where the sun had split it. Halfway down he could see the water through gaps between boards, moving slow and dark, not clear like a pool. Not friendly. Just there.

The dock reached out into the cove like a finger. The boards near the end were lighter from sun, darker near the waterline where algae had stained them. A rope was coiled over a cleat in neat circles. A minnow bucket hung from another rope, bumping the dock post with each small swell.

Matt leaned over to look at the bucket.

"Don't," Brian said, not loud, but final.

"Why?"

"Because it'll swing and you'll go in after it," Brian said. "And you don't go in under docks."

His father's voice carried from the porch. "Nobody in the fishing well."

The words didn't come with explanation. They didn't need it. Matt looked down where the boards cut a square in the dock and saw the hinged lid of the fishing well, stained darker than the rest. It was closed.

Scott crouched and put his hand flat on the lid like he could feel something inside.

"It's alive in there," Matt whispered, even though he didn't know if that was true.

Scott shrugged without looking at him.

Brian moved to the edge where the ladder was and sat down carefully, one foot testing the first rung. The lake slapped the metal with a small, steady sound. Tap. Tap. Tap.

Matt watched Brian like he always did.

"You can go in from the side," Scott said. "Not behind the boat."

There was no boat in the water yet. The rule existed anyway.

Matt stepped to the edge and sat down. The boards were hot against the backs of his thighs. He lowered one foot into the water and jerked it back.

Cold.

Not mountain cold. Just lake cold, deep and sudden, like it didn't care what the air felt like.

His brothers laughed at him, not meanly. Just because it was funny to see him flinch.

He forced himself to lower his foot again, then the other. The water climbed his shins. It tugged at the hairs on his legs. It smelled like algae and gasoline and something muddy.

"Quit splashing," Brian said.

"I'm not," he lied.

Scott slid in without making a sound. Brian followed, quieter than Matt expected. They moved away from the dock in practiced strokes, not showing off, not rushing. Matt kicked hard, trying to keep up, water filling his ears, the sound of the world dropping away.

Under the dock it was darker. He could see the white foam floats beneath the boards, scarred and pitted. Light broke into long green ribbons that moved when the dock shifted.

He pushed himself forward and then stopped. The dark felt like a mouth.

Scott surfaced beside him. "Don't go under there," he said, eyes wide like he'd already seen something and wasn't going to say it.

Matt nodded, relieved to have a rule.

They swam out into the cove instead, where the water warmed against their shoulders. The dock drifted behind them. The cabin sat back under the trees like it was watching, windows black in the afternoon light.

When they climbed out, dripping and breathing hard, his father was at the end of the dock with a tool box open. He didn't look up right away. He tightened something on the cleat and tested it with a tug.

"Towel," his mother called from the porch.

Matt grabbed the first towel he could reach. It was scratchy and smelled like the cabin.

He wrapped it around himself and stood barefoot on the boards. The dock tapped once under his heel, then again, and he felt the movement travel up through his legs.

He didn't know what the cabin meant. Not yet.

He only knew that the water was darker than he expected and that everyone spoke differently here—shorter, quieter, like words cost more.

CH 03

First Night Rules

BY EVENING, the cabin had its own noise. The screen door slapped. The ceiling fan clicked once each time it turned, a tired sound. Somebody's footsteps made the same board complain every time they crossed the room. Plates clinked in the sink. Outside, the cicadas kept going, as if they had no way to stop.

Brian watched it all without looking like he was watching.

His father carried things in and set them down where they belonged. Not where there was space. Where they belonged. Tackle box on the counter. Boat keys on the nail by the door. Knife in the drawer that stuck unless you lifted it first. It wasn't instruction. It was possession.

"Close that," his father said when Matt left the screen door half-open.

Matt shut it hard enough to make the frame rattle.

"Not like that," his father said.

He said it like there was a right way to close a door that mattered.

Brian filed the rule away. Quiet hands. Quiet feet. Quiet everything.

His mother moved between rooms with a dish towel over her shoulder. She wiped counters that didn't need wiping. She checked the windows even though the air outside was still hot. When she looked out, she looked down toward the dock first.

His father ate standing up, leaning against the counter as if sitting would make him soft. Afterward he walked the cabin like he was checking for things that could go wrong.

Brian followed without being told.

His father stopped at the back door and slid the deadbolt into place. Then he checked it again, pulling once on the handle.

"Why do you lock it?" Matt asked.

His father didn't answer right away. He looked at Matt as if he didn't know whether the question was serious.

"Because," he said finally.

Brian's jaw tightened. Matt always wanted reasons. Brian had learned early that reasons were rare.

His father moved to the porch and stood there, scanning the yard, the line of trees, the darkening shape of the lake beyond them. He didn't look afraid. He looked responsible.

Brian wanted that look.

* * *

After supper, his father carried a coffee can down to the seawall.

Not coffee inside it. Kindling. Splinters. Paper. Things that had to be burned because there was no place to put them where they wouldn't come back.

The stones were already there in a rough ring, half sunk in dirt and leaf litter. Someone had made it years ago and then every summer added to it without thinking.

Brian followed with Scott and Matt, because following was what you did. Their mother came last with a dish towel over her shoulder and a flashlight in her hand even though there was still a stripe of light left in the sky.

The fire caught fast. Paper folded in on itself and turned black. Twigs snapped and glowed. Smoke rose straight up at first and then drifted sideways when the wind changed.

Matt found a stick and started poking at the edge like it was a job. He liked jobs you could see.

"Don't wave it," Brian said.

Matt froze, then moved the stick slower, offended.

Across the cove, a dock light blinked on. Bugs gathered around it immediately, a small cloud that looked like ash before it became insects.

Their father sat on an upside-down bucket and held a beer in one hand, elbow on his knee. He didn't talk much. He watched the fire and listened to the lake the way he listened to weather.

Their mother stood, not sitting down, as if sitting would mean the day was finished. She shone the flashlight once at the dark waterline and then turned it off again, satisfied.

"You remember when Earl brought that old stove down here?" their father said finally, voice low.

Their mother made a sound that could have been agreement.

Brian didn't know Earl yet as a person. He knew him as a name that meant grown men and family obligations and leaving the lake in the dark because someone said you had to.

"That thing almost took three of us," their father said, and he smiled without teeth.

Matt perked up. "How?"

Their father didn't answer right away. He stared into the fire like he was watching the story arrange itself.

"It slid," he said. "Right off the trailer. We were idiots. We thought we could muscle it. Your grandpa said no and we didn't listen."

Scott looked up at the word grandpa as if it was a tool he could hold.

Brian watched his father's hands. They were big, knuckles rough, the kind of hands that could do things and then refuse to explain them.

Matt said, "Did it break?"

"It broke the trailer," their father said. "Not the stove."

Matt laughed, relieved by the idea of something surviving.

Their mother finally sat on the seawall, dish towel still on her shoulder, and stretched her legs out. She didn't add anything to the story. She didn't correct it. She let it be what it was, a thing adults said to each other while kids learned how danger could be turned into a joke.

Across the water, someone's radio came on low. A song floated in and out between waves and engine noise.

Brian stared into the fire until his eyes watered from the smoke. He told himself it was only smoke.

He could feel rules forming around the heat. Don't get too close. Don't talk too loud. Don't ask for more than the story wants to give you.

When the coffee can was empty, their father stood and nudged the burning paper deeper with the toe of his boot.

"All right," he said.

They went back up to the cabin in a line, smoke caught in their hair, the screen door slapping behind them like a warning.

Later, when the light was gone and the cabin held only the yellow circle of the lamp in the living room, Matt started in on the candy.

Not asking. Just taking.

He grabbed a handful of wrapped pieces from the bowl on the table and shoved two into his pockets before anyone could stop him.

"Hey," Brian said.

Matt froze, guilty already, chin lifted in defiance anyway. "What?"

"Mom said two," Scott murmured from the couch.

His mother hadn't said anything. But Scott always heard the rule even when it wasn't spoken.

"She didn't," Matt snapped.

His father didn't look up from the paper. He was reading it like the words mattered, even though it was yesterday's news.

Brian stepped closer to the table. Not fast. Not angry. Just close enough that Matt had to decide whether to back up.

"Put them back," he said.

"Why do you care?" Matt asked, voice rising.

Brian cared because noise drew attention. Because his father would look up and something would harden. Because rules mattered here even when you couldn't name them.

"Just do it," he said.

Matt's face worked, pride fighting obedience. Then he dropped the candy back into the bowl, wrappers making a small plastic sound too loud in the quiet room.

His father turned a page. The paper crackled. He didn't say anything. That was the reward.

When they finally went to bed, the three of them in the same room, the air was thick and still. The sheets smelled like cabinet wood. Matt kept moving, knees bumping, trying to find space where there wasn't any.

"Stop," Brian whispered.

"I can't," Matt whispered back.

Scott lay on his back, hands folded on his stomach, listening to the fan click and the dock tap somewhere below the windows, a small sound that made the night feel awake.

Outside, a boat engine rose and fell on the channel, too far to see, close enough to hear.

Brian stared at the ceiling where the light from the living room lamp leaked under the doorframe in a thin line. He listened for his parents' voices. They were in the kitchen, quiet, words too low to catch.

He wanted to know what they were saying.

He didn't ask.

When Matt finally stopped moving and Scott's breathing slowed, Brian slid out of bed and stood barefoot on the cool floor.

He opened the bedroom door just enough to widen the line of light. The hall smelled like damp wood and dish soap. From the kitchen came their parents' voices—low, steady, the words smoothing into each other until they weren't words anymore.

Brian walked to the back door and put his fingers on the deadbolt. It was slid over. He pulled once on the handle anyway.

He stood there a moment, listening, then eased back into the room and closed the door until the latch clicked soft.

Matt had kicked the sheet down. Brian pulled it back over his knees without waking him.

He lay down and watched the thin line of light under the door until it went dull, then darker.

CH 04

Good Order

On Sunday morning, Rick stood in the kitchen with his keys in his hand and said, "We should go to Our Lady."
The sentence hung there like it belonged to a different decade.

Linda looked up from the counter. Her face didn't change, but her eyes did—quick, careful, already deciding whether to correct him or let it pass. Owen sat at the table with his phone in his lap, screen glowing against his thumbs. Matt watched his father's mouth as if the words might keep coming out wrong.

Rick blinked and shook his head once. "Church," he said, and the correction sounded like a tool dropped back into place.

Sunday morning, they went to Our Lady of the Lake.

The church sat back from the road with a small sign out front and a gravel lot full of cars that looked older than the lake brochures—sedans with sun-faded paint, a few trucks with coolers in the bed, one long car that gleamed like it wanted attention.

Inside, the air was cooler than outside and smelled like old wood and wax. A ceiling fan turned and made a soft clicking sound each time it came around. People slid into pews and the kneelers dropped in uneven thumps, row after row.

Matt sat between his brothers and tried to keep his legs still. Brian sat straight, hands folded like he was being watched. Scott watched everything—the aisle, the side doors, the way adults moved without looking like they were moving.

Their mother dipped her fingers in the holy water and touched Matt's forehead, quick and practiced, then moved on to Scott. Their father did the same without speaking, his hand steady, as if this was a rule he understood.

When the priest's voice rose, it rose with the room. When it fell, it fell into the quiet of people breathing and pages turning. Matt didn't understand most of the words, but he understood the shape of it: stand, sit, kneel, answer when everyone else answered.

On the way out, sunlight hit hard and made Matt squint. Their father paused on the steps and looked down at the lake through the trees for half a second like he was checking it, then turned back to the car.

***

Back at the cabin, the bikes waited in the shade beside the porch.

Banana seats cracked and sun-faded. Chrome sissy bars bent just slightly out of true. One set of handlebars rose high like antlers. Another was straight, the grips worn smooth. Matt's front reflector was gone. No one bothered to replace it.

Brian's chain was oiled. You could hear the difference.

"Let's go," Brian said, already swinging his leg over.

Matt followed too fast and almost kicked the pedal. He caught himself and acted like he meant to do it. Scott adjusted his seat with both hands, careful, like he could make the bike behave if he treated it right.

They pushed off down the gravel, tires crunching, and the cabin dropped behind them quickly. The road was narrow and the sun hit it hard in spots where trees opened. In the shade, the air was cooler and smelled like damp leaves and clay. In the sun, it smelled like hot asphalt and dust.

Matt stood up on the pedals and let the bike wobble, just to feel it.

"Quit," Brian said without turning around.

Matt sat back down, cheeks hot.

They rode faster anyway.

The joy came first, the simple fact of speed. Wind against his face. The chain rattle. The rise and fall of his breath matching the turns. His legs burned in a good way. His stomach lifted each time they coasted down a slope.

They didn't talk much when they rode. Talking was for when you stopped.

Brian kept to the edge of the road, too close to the drop-off in places where the ground fell away into brush and rock. He did it like it was nothing. Like he knew the road personally.

Scott watched the curves. He counted them without moving his mouth, eyes tracking the way the road tightened before you could see what was coming.

Matt watched his brothers more than he watched the road.

When the truck came, it came too fast.

They heard it first—engine strain, then the hiss of tires on gravel at the shoulder. Brian swerved without thinking, bike leaning hard, front wheel skittering. Matt jerked his handlebars and felt his tire slide.

The truck blasted past, close enough that the wind of it slapped his shirt against his ribs. A man's arm hung out the window. He didn't wave. He didn't slow.

Matt's heart hammered so hard he could taste it.

They didn't stop.

They kept riding until the road narrowed into a path that wasn't a path, just dirt worn down by feet and tires and stubbornness. Branches reached in and scraped their arms. Leaves slapped their faces. The woods closed around them the way the cabin never did.

Brian lifted his front wheel over a root without slowing. Scott followed, careful. Matt hit the root and bounced hard, teeth clicking. He swallowed a yelp.

"You okay?" Scott asked.

Matt nodded. He wasn't sure.

They rode until they couldn't ride anymore and had to push their bikes through brush, the tires catching on vines. The ground was loose limestone and leaf litter that hid holes. Cicadas droned even louder here, or maybe it just sounded louder because there was no other noise.

Brian stopped where the trees opened onto a small clearing. Nothing special. Just a spot where sunlight reached the ground and the air smelled different.

"Here," he said.

Matt didn't know what here meant, but he liked the way Brian said it, like he'd claimed something.

They dropped their bikes and lay back in the grass, sweat cooling on their backs. Matt stared up at the branches above him, the sky cut into pieces. A bird called somewhere high and then went quiet.

Scott picked up a stick and drew a line in the dirt. Then another. Not a map. Just a way of thinking with his hands.

Brian closed his eyes.

For a few minutes, it was only heat and breath and the feeling that the world was theirs because they could reach it.

Then Matt sat up. "We should go farther."

Brian opened his eyes and looked at him like he was measuring something. "We will," he said.

On the ride back, Matt watched the road for trucks.

None came.

That almost made it worse. It meant the danger didn't have to announce itself.

When the cabin came back into view through the trees, his mother was on the porch, hands on her hips. Not angry. Just waiting.

"Where were you?" she asked.

Brian didn't answer right away. He lifted his bike and walked it up the steps like he hadn't heard.

"Around," Brian said finally.

His mother looked at Matt's scraped knee then, a thin line of red that hadn't been there when they left. Matt pulled his leg back automatically.

His mother didn't ask how it happened.

She said, "Wash up," and went back inside.

They rolled their bikes into the shade beside the porch again. Matt leaned his bike carefully so it wouldn't fall and make noise.

Scott looked at him and didn't say anything.

Matt understood anyway.

Some things stayed in the woods.

Ch 05

The Cool Air

A FEW DAYS into the trip, Scott found it because he was always looking down.
Not on purpose. Just the way his eyes went to the ground and the edges of things. Gravel in the road. A nail half-buried near the steps. A place where the limestone had crumbled and left a clean pale seam.

They were on the bikes again, the three of them, pushing past where the path wanted to stop. Brian rode first like he'd been born on a slope. Matt rode last because he couldn't keep the pace and because Brian said so.

It was late afternoon and the heat sat low in the woods. The air smelled like leaf mold and crushed leaves. Their tires made a soft hiss over dirt and small stones. Cicadas throbbed in a constant sheet.

The path narrowed against a bluff of rock that rose out of the trees, rough and gray, streaked with darker water lines from rain. Brian slowed and stood up on the pedals, scanning ahead as if he expected something to step out.

"This is nothing," Matt said, breathy, trying to make it sound like he wasn't tired.

"Shut up," Brian said, not angry, just cutting it off.

Scott rode close to the rock because there was less brush there. His handlebars brushed leaves. Something scratched his knuckles.

Then he felt it.

Not a touch. A change.

Cold air, slipping out of the stone like a slow breath.

He braked hard enough that his back tire skidded. Dirt sprayed. Brian swung his head around.

"What?" he said.

Scott didn't answer right away. He leaned his bike against a tree and walked to the rock. His palm hovered just above it. The air was different there. Cooler. Damp. He could smell it—wet rock, something old and sour, like a basement.

Matt rolled up behind them and almost tipped over, catching himself with a foot. "What is it?" he said, already smiling like it was a prize.

Scott crouched. Between two slabs of limestone there was a narrow dark gap, half-hidden by vines. If you weren't looking for it, it read as shadow.

He pushed the vine aside with one finger.

The gap went back farther than it should have.

He knocked once on the rock beside it with his knuckle. The sound came back wrong—hollow, not solid. It carried inward and then disappeared.

Brian stepped closer, expression hardening. He didn't like things that didn't behave.

"It's a cave," Matt whispered, as if saying it out loud would close it.

"It's not," Brian said automatically.

Scott didn't move. He tilted his head and listened.

Drip.

Not from the trees. From inside.

"It's something," Scott said.

Brian leaned down, put his ear near the gap without putting his hand in. He stayed that way a moment, still as a dog listening.

When he straightened, he didn't smile.

"Don't tell Mom," he said.

"Why not?" Matt asked, immediate and loud.

Brian looked at him the way he looked at the screen door when it slammed. "Because," he said.

Scott watched Brian's mouth when he said it. The word didn't mean explanation. It meant ownership.

Brian grabbed a stick and broke it down to a shorter length, snapping it with his hands until he had a straight piece. He used it to pry the vines wider, to push at the loose dirt at the entrance. The stick came away damp.

"I'm going in," Matt said.

"No," Brian said.

Matt's face went still. His pride always arrived first, before fear. "Why do you get to—"

"Because I said," Brian said, and the sound of it made the woods feel smaller.

Scott could feel the cold air on his face now. It raised goosebumps on his forearms.

Brian lowered himself to the ground and put one shoulder toward the gap. He tested it the way he tested the dock ladder: slow, careful, weight first. Limestone scraped softly against his shirt. He sucked in a breath to narrow his chest and slid through.

His feet disappeared. Then his legs. Then his hips. He paused when only his back and shoulders were visible, one hand braced on the rock.

"If you get stuck," Scott said.

Brian turned his head just enough to look back. "I'm not," he said, and pulled the rest of himself inside.

Scott leaned toward the opening and listened hard.

There was shuffling. A small cough. The scrape of shoe rubber on rock.

Then Brian's voice, muffled. "It goes."

Matt edged closer and tried to look in. The darkness swallowed his eyes. He could only see the faint pale blur of the rock a foot inside.

"Let me," Matt said, voice rising.

"No," Scott said before he could stop himself.

Matt stared at him, surprised by the refusal.

Scott heard himself breathe. He could smell the cave on his breath now, as if it had already gotten inside him.

Brian came back out backward, bracing his palms on the rock, sliding his shoulders through. His hair was damp at the roots. He blinked hard like the light hurt.

"It's narrow," he said. "But it opens up."

"How far?" Scott asked.

Brian shrugged once. "Far enough."

Matt bounced on his toes. "Let me go. I'll fit better."

Brian looked past him toward the cabin's direction, even though you couldn't see it from here. He looked as if he could still feel his father's eyes from miles away.

"We go together," he said finally. "And nobody talks."

Matt nodded too fast.

Scott didn't nod. He was already measuring. The width of the gap. The angle of the rock. How much sky you'd lose once you went inside.

"If Mom calls," Matt whispered, as if it was a joke, but his eyes were bright.

Brian ignored him. He broke off another stick and shoved it into the dirt at the entrance, angled like a marker.

"So we don't miss it," he said.

Scott thought, So we can pretend we didn't.

* * *

The three of them left the bikes hidden off the path in brush that scratched their shins. Brian made Matt tuck his shirt in so it wouldn't snag. Matt did it, annoyed, then forgot and pulled it out again. Brian shoved it back in without speaking.

Scott went last because he wanted to see what it looked like from outside before it swallowed them.

Inside, the air changed immediately.

The sound of the woods dropped away like someone had shut a door. Cicadas became a distant vibration. Their breathing got loud.

The rock at the entrance was cool against his shoulder when he squeezed through. It pressed into the bone. The limestone smelled wet and faintly metallic. He could taste it.

Brian went first again. He moved with his hands out in front of him, fingers touching rock, testing. Matt came next, too eager, bumping into Brian's heel.

"Slow," Brian said.

"I am," Matt said, lying.

The passage sloped downward and then leveled out. Scott's shoes slid on slick stone. He put his palm down once and felt grit and damp. When he lifted it, his hand was darkened with wet limestone dust.

Drip.

The sound was steady, patient.

Farther in, the rock opened enough that he could straighten his back. The ceiling rose higher than he expected. He lifted his head and couldn't see the top clearly. The dark wasn't a color. It was thickness.

Brian stopped and held up one hand.

Matt froze behind him, breathing fast.

"Listen," Brian whispered.

Scott listened until his ears felt full.

There was the drip. And something else. A thin running sound, like water moving somewhere it didn't want to be heard.

Matt whispered, "It's a river."

Brian didn't answer.

Scott could smell something sharp now—bat, maybe, or just old damp. He didn't know. He didn't want to know.

Brian stepped forward again and the floor changed under his feet, shifting from slick stone to packed dirt. Scott felt it too when he moved: softer ground, a little give.

Matt reached out and brushed his hand along the wall, making a slow scraping sound. Brian turned and slapped his hand away, quick and hard, not hurting, just warning.

Matt glared in the dark. "What?"

"Quiet," Brian said.

Scott thought of his father saying it in the cabin. Close that. Not like that. Quiet hands. He felt the same tightening in his stomach, the same urge to do it right.

They moved until the light from the entrance was only a pale suggestion behind them. Scott could no longer see leaves. The cave took the woods away.

Matt started to hum without noticing. Just a small sound. Brian stopped and turned.

"Stop," he said.

The humming cut off.

They stood in the dark and listened again, all three of them holding their breath like that would make them invisible.

Scott reached into his pocket and found the small cheap flashlight he'd taken off the kitchen table earlier without asking. It was a penlight with a worn metal clip. He clicked it once.

Nothing.

His throat tightened.

He clicked it again, harder, thumb pressing until it hurt.

A weak yellow circle blinked on and steadied.

The beam hit the wall and made the rock look alive—ridges, holes, places where water had cut channels. He swung the light and caught scratches in the stone that weren't natural.

Letters.

Not careful. Just carved deep enough to stay.

BOB

Under it, another name, half gone.

And a date that didn't mean anything to him.

Brian leaned in close, face lit from below. "Somebody's been here," he said, as if it was an accusation.

"So?" Matt whispered, excited again.

Scott moved the light lower and saw a pile of old beer cans in a dry pocket of dirt, crushed flat, the pull tabs still attached. He felt a sudden heat in his cheeks, like he'd walked in on adults being sloppy.

"They're old," Matt said, disappointed.

Brian stared at them a long moment. Then he looked back toward the entrance, the light behind them like a thin exit.

"We don't touch anything," he said.

Scott nodded.

Matt opened his mouth and then shut it again.

They went a little farther, not much. Brian chose the direction. Scott kept track anyway. Left where the wall pinched. Right where the floor dipped. Three steps up over a rock. A low ceiling where you had to duck and feel the stone pass close over your head.

He memorized it like a route home.

At one point Matt's shoe slid and his knee hit rock. The sound echoed hard.

He froze, hand on his knee.

Brian didn't yell. He didn't need to. He just stared at him until Matt's face flushed in the flashlight beam.

"Sorry," Matt whispered, and the word sounded wrong in that place.

Scott saw a small white thing on the ground near his shoe and bent down. A piece of bone, maybe. Or a shell. He didn't know. He didn't pick it up. He just looked until his eyes tried to make it into something harmless.

The drip continued.

Scott realized, all at once, that if someone outside shouted their names, the sound would not get in here fast. That the cave could hold them in the same way the cabin held smells and years.

He swallowed.

Brian turned back toward the entrance like he'd decided the same thing without saying it.

"Out," he said.

Matt started to protest and then didn't.

On the way back the passage felt tighter. Scott could feel rock against both shoulders at once. He could hear his own breath and Matt's quick breaths ahead of him, Brian's steadier breathing in front.

When the light at the entrance finally widened into daylight, his eyes stung. He slid through the gap and stood up too fast, dizzy.

The woods hit him with noise again—cicadas, birds, wind in leaves—like it had been waiting.

Brian stepped out last and turned immediately, pushing vines back into place with careful hands until the rock looked like rock again.

He snapped the marker stick in half and shoved it under a leaf pile.

Matt watched, mouth open. "How are we gonna find it?"

Brian looked at him. "We will," he said.

Scott felt the damp of the cave still on his skin. He looked at the rock and tried to see the gap again.

Once you knew where it was, you couldn't unsee it.

* * *

Back at the cabin, their mother was at the sink, hands in soapy water. The sound of the faucet filled the kitchen. The radio played low on the counter, a man's voice talking about nothing important.

Their father was outside on the porch with a hammer, tapping at a board that had come loose near the steps. Tap. Tap. Tap. Small work, done without comment.

"Where'd you go?" their mother asked without turning around.

Brian leaned his bike against the porch rail in the same spot as always. He didn't look at her. "Just around," he said.

Their mother's hands paused in the water for a second. Not because she didn't believe him. Because she knew it was the only answer she was going to get.

She rinsed a plate and set it in the rack. "Dinner in a bit," she said, and kept washing.

Matt hovered, itching to tell. His eyes kept flicking to Brian. Brian didn't give him permission.

Scott walked past them into the bedroom and shut the door gently. He took the penlight out of his pocket and held it in his hand a moment, feeling the dampness of his own sweat on the metal.

He opened the top drawer of the dresser where they kept things that didn't have a place and pushed the penlight under a folded towel so it wouldn't be seen.

In the bottom of his other pocket, a small bit of limestone grit scratched his finger when he moved.

He rubbed it between thumb and forefinger until it crumbled.

Then he washed his hands longer than he needed to, standing at the sink in the back room where no one watched, the water running cold over his knuckles.

He kept rinsing until he couldn't smell the cave anymore.

CH 06

Coffee Grounds

LATER THAT WEEK, the box behind the cabin started as a dare. "Worms," Brian said, like it was obvious. He said it the way his father said roof or oil or rope—things you dealt with before they became trouble.

Matt made a face. "Gross."

Scott squinted at the ground where the shade stayed damp. "They'll crawl out."

"Then we keep the lid on," Brian said.

He'd found an old wooden crate in the shed with slats missing and nails bent over. He dragged it out into the strip of shade behind the cabin where the air smelled like wet leaves and something faintly sour, like old coffee left too long in a pot.

Their mother watched from the porch with a dish towel over her shoulder. She didn't tell them not to. She only said, "Don't dump it near the steps."

Brian took that as permission.

He lined the crate with a cardboard box flattened and folded until it fit. The cardboard was soft from damp, edges fraying. He poured coffee grounds from a can into the bottom, the smell sharp and bitter. Then he layered in grass clippings that stuck to his fingers and a handful of kitchen scraps their mother handed him without comment—potato peels, a bruised banana, an onion skin that made his eyes water.

Matt poked at the pile with a stick. "It's gonna stink."

"It already stinks," Brian said.

Scott stood back, arms crossed, watching the way Brian's hands moved. He always worked like he was building something that mattered, even when it didn't.

Brian wiped his palms on his shorts and went to the cooler by the porch steps. He lifted the lid like he was opening a treasure chest.

Inside, under ice, were worms.

Nightcrawlers almost as long as his forearm, thick and slick, coiled in damp dirt. Red wigglers smaller, squirming fast. Matt leaned in and then recoiled.

"Where'd you get those?" Scott asked.

Brian didn't look up. "From Dad," he said.

It wasn't a lie exactly. Their father had bought them, or had always had them, or had told them where they went. Brian took things that belonged to the cabin and treated them like tools.

He grabbed a handful and dropped them into the crate. They hit the coffee grounds and disappeared immediately, burying themselves as if the air hurt.

Matt made a sound in his throat. "Ugh."

"Quit," Brian said, and kept working.

By the time the lid went on—a piece of scrap plywood weighted with a rock—Brian's forehead was sweating. The shade didn't cool you so much as it kept the sun off your shoulders.

He stood back and looked at the crate the way he looked at his bike chain after he oiled it.

"There," he said.

Scott waited. He knew there was always a second part.

Brian wiped his hands again. "We can sell them."

"To who?" Matt asked.

Brian nodded toward the water you couldn't see through the trees. "People."

Matt brightened immediately. He was already picturing a cold soda bottle and a box of sparklers without having to ask for either.

Scott said, "They'll die."

"Not if we keep it right," Brian said, already listing tasks in his head. "You water it. Not too much. You," he pointed at Scott, "you keep count. How many we got. How many go out."

Scott's stomach dipped. He looked at Brian's hands, already dirty with coffee grounds and damp cardboard, and then down at his own, clean.

"Why me?" he asked.

"Because you'll do it right," Brian said, like it was a compliment.

Matt bounced on his heels. "How much do we charge?"

Brian didn't answer. He looked toward the porch again as if checking whether their mother could hear him, even though she wasn't listening in that way. Their father's voice carried from somewhere inside the cabin, a drawer sliding, the sound of metal tools shifting.

Brian lowered his voice anyway. "We can take them to Alhonna."

Scott knew the name. He'd heard it said like a destination, not a place. Alhonna meant minnows and soda and tourists with pale legs, and the road there with blind curves where trucks came fast.

Matt said, "We can ride."

Brian nodded once. He'd already decided.

* * *

Two days later, Brian held a fistful of damp dirt and worms over the crate and let the soil run through his fingers slowly.

They were alive.

The worms had multiplied in a way that felt wrong, too fast. If you lifted the cardboard, they were everywhere, twisting through coffee grounds, threading between banana peel and grass, escaping toward the edges where light seeped in.

Matt complained about watering because he complained about everything that wasn't fun. Scott had filled a notebook page with numbers that meant nothing to anyone else.

"You're writing it down?" Matt said, disgusted.

"He's keeping count," Brian said.

"Worm count," Matt muttered, and snickered.

Brian didn't laugh. He wasn't in it for jokes.

That afternoon, their father handed Brian two bills folded tight.

"Get minnows," he said. "Two scoops. And a pack of hooks."

Brian took the money with both hands like it was something you could tear. He didn't ask questions. That was part of why their father trusted him.

Their father looked at the other two boys. "You go with him," he said. "Stay off the highway."

"We will," Brian said before either of them could.

Their mother stood at the sink rinsing dishes. She didn't turn around. She said, "Be back before dark."

Brian nodded, even though she couldn't see it.

Outside, the bikes waited in the shade. Brian checked his tires with his thumb like he knew what it should feel like. Matt bounced his front wheel once and smiled at the sound of it.

Scott tucked the folded bills into Brian's shirt pocket himself, making sure it sat flat.

Brian didn't say thank you. He only said, "Don't talk in there."

"In where?" Matt asked.

"At Alhonna," Brian said. "Let me."

Scott understood. He'd watched adults look past kids like they were furniture until the kids spoke. Then adults remembered they were there and got sharper.

They rode out on the gravel road that ran behind the cabins. The sun hit them hard in open spots, then disappeared under tree cover again. Their tires threw small stones. Brian led, shoulders squared, pedaling steady. Matt lagged and then sprinted to catch up, making it a game.

When the road curved near a blind rise, Scott heard the engine before he saw it and felt his skin tighten.

He held up a hand without thinking. "Truck."

Brian slowed. Matt didn't, not right away. He came up behind them fast and had to brake hard, back tire skidding.

"Idiot," Brian said under his breath.

The truck crested the rise and passed too close, wind pushing their shirts against their ribs. The driver didn't wave. Gravel spit against their shins.

Matt sucked in air and laughed like it was funny.

Scott didn't laugh.

When they reached Alhonna, the lake opened up between trees and the buildings appeared like a small town that had decided to pretend it was a resort. There were boats tied to the dock, their hulls knocking softly. The air smelled like gasoline and sunscreen.

Inside the store, it was cooler. A bait fridge hummed loud enough to feel in your teeth. Minnows swam in metal tanks under fluorescent light, their bodies flashing silver as they turned.

Soda bottles sat in wire racks, sweating. Labels bright. Glass thick.

Behind the counter, a man with sunburned arms looked up as the doorbell clinked.

He stared at them a beat too long, then nodded at Brian like he knew his face.

"You boys lost?" he asked.

Brian stepped forward, voice steady. "No sir. Dad sent us."

"Which dad?" the man asked, not smiling.

Brian didn't hesitate. He said their father's name like it was a password.

The man's eyes shifted, measuring, then he grunted once and turned toward the minnows. "Two scoops?"

"Yes sir," Brian said.

Matt drifted toward the soda rack, eyes fixed on the bottles. Scott watched the man's hands as he dipped a metal scoop into the tank, minnows flickering against the mesh. Water dripped onto the counter. The smell was sharp, fish and wet metal.

The man slid the bait bucket across. "Hooks?"

Brian nodded. "Small."

The man grabbed a pack off a pegboard and set it down. He said a price.

Brian reached into his pocket and pulled out the folded bills. He set them on the counter flat. Neat. He didn't fumble.

The man counted slowly, eyes on the bills like he didn't trust paper. Then he opened the register and made change.

Coins clinked into the tray. The sound felt loud.

Matt reached for a soda bottle.

Brian's hand shot out and caught his wrist without looking. Not hard. Just final.

Matt glared.

The man watched them a moment, then said, "You want one, you pay for it."

Brian nodded like he'd expected that rule. He looked down at the change in his palm.

It was only coins. Not much.

"One," Brian said.

Matt's face lit up like he'd been forgiven.

The man took the coins and slid a bottle across the counter. The glass was cold and wet. Matt held it like it might break.

Outside, Brian made Matt carry the bait bucket with both hands.

"Don't spill it," he said.

"I'm not," Matt said, shoulders hunched under the weight.

Scott watched Brian tuck the remaining change into his pocket without counting it again. He'd already counted. He'd already decided where it went.

They rode back with the bait bucket sloshing and the soda bottle clinking softly against Matt's teeth when he drank too fast. The road felt narrower on the way home. The sun was lower, light slanting through trees.

Near the last curve, Matt swerved to avoid a branch and almost dumped the bucket.

Brian reached out and steadied it with one hand while still riding.

"Jesus," Scott breathed, surprised by the word coming out of him.

Brian didn't look back. "Quiet," he said.

At the cabin, their father took the bait bucket and looked inside like he was checking their work. He didn't ask about the soda.

Brian handed him the hooks and then laid the remaining change on the counter in a small pile, exact and clean.

Their father nodded once, satisfied.

Brian stood there a moment longer, hands at his sides, face blank, waiting for the next instruction.

Scott watched the small pile of coins on the counter and knew, without seeing it, that Brian had kept something back.

He didn't say anything.

Outside, behind the cabin, the worm box sat under its rock-weighted lid, dark and damp, working without anyone watching it.

* * *

The next morning, before anyone else was fully up, Scott went behind the cabin and lifted the rock.

The plywood was damp underneath. The smell rose immediately—coffee grounds gone sour, banana peel sweetening, earth warm and alive.

Worms moved in the dark like threads being pulled.

He put the lid back fast, guilty without knowing why, and stood there listening to the cabin wake. A drawer slid. The fridge hummed. Somewhere out on the channel an engine started and ran steady.

By the time Brian came out, he already had a coffee can in his hand.

"We're selling," Brian said.

Matt stumbled out behind him rubbing his eyes, hair sticking up. "To who?"

Brian nodded toward the dock. "Somebody."

They carried the coffee can down the steps. Scott held it with both hands, careful, feeling the weight shift when something inside moved. Brian walked ahead like he was leading them into town again. Matt lagged, still half asleep, then jogged to catch up.

On the next dock over, a man sat in a lawn chair with a fishing pole propped against the rail. He wore a sun-faded hat and had a beer in a foam sleeve even though the sun was barely up.

Brian didn't hesitate.

"Mister," he called, polite and too loud.

The man turned his head slowly like he didn't like being summoned. His eyes went from Brian's face to the coffee can in Scott's hands. "What," he said.

Brian lifted his chin. "Worms," he said. "We got good ones."

Matt brightened, suddenly invested. "Nightcrawlers," he added, like he knew what he was talking about.

The man stared at them a long beat, then looked down at his own bait bucket, already full of store-bought worms in a plastic cup with a lid.

He said, "No," and went back to his line.

Matt's face tightened. "He didn't even look," he whispered, outraged.

Brian's jaw worked. He started to speak again and then stopped.

Scott felt heat climb his neck. He wanted to back away. He also wanted to be paid for the thing they'd made.

From farther down the cove, another boat idled past slow, leaving a small wake that tapped their dock once. A man at the helm lifted a hand in a half wave without looking closely.

Brian raised his voice at the passing boat. "Worms!" he called.

The man didn't turn. The boat kept moving.

Matt laughed once, sharp. "This is stupid."

Brian turned on him. "You're stupid," he said, and the sentence landed harder than it needed to.

Matt's mouth opened, then shut. His face went hot.

Scott held the coffee can and watched the dock boards. He could feel the worms moving under the lid like a secret.

Behind them, the screen door at their cabin slapped.

Linda stood on the porch with her coffee in her hand, watching. She didn't yell. She didn't hurry down.

She only said, "Bring that back up here," and her voice carried clean over the water like a rule.

Brian froze, offended, as if she'd taken something from him.

Matt said, "We were just—"

Linda didn't let him finish. "Bring it back," she repeated.

They carried the coffee can back up the steps, slower now.

At the top, Linda took it from Scott's hands and held it like it weighed nothing. She set it on the porch boards and put her palm on the lid.

"You don't go bothering people on their docks," she said. "Not for money. Not for attention."

Brian stared at her, jaw set. "We weren't bothering," he said.

Linda looked at him a long moment and Scott saw what she chose not to say—about beer at sunrise, about men who didn't want to be reminded of children, about the way docks were private even when the lake wasn't.

She only said, "You want to fish, you fish. You want to sell something, you ask your father first."

Brian didn't answer.

Matt muttered, "Fine," like he'd been punished.

Scott stood still, hands empty, and felt the shame of it settle on him as if it were his.

Linda picked up the coffee can again and carried it toward the back of the cabin. "Put the rock back on," she called over her shoulder.

Scott went behind the cabin and set the rock down on the plywood lid.

The thud was solid and final.

Ch 07

Five Cents

AFTER JULIE FINALLY got Jake and Emily inside, Scott carried the trash bag down to the seawall and felt the weight of it pull his shoulder.

Inside were cans and bottles from the drive and supper—aluminum light until it wasn't, glass clinking when it hit his leg. The fire was already going, small flames licking at kindling, smoke finding its way into his hair.

The cans shifted and clinked again, a bright sound that didn't fit the dark.

He'd offered to take it because the cabin kitchen had started to feel too tight—Julie counting time, Brian counting tasks, everyone pretending the counting wasn't fear.

Scott went early because the cans were still there then.

After breakfast, after boats started up, after the sun got high, the shore got crowded and the cans disappeared into trash bags adults tied off and forgot. But in the first light, before anyone wanted to see what they'd done the night before, the cans sat where they'd been dropped.

On Sundays, if the lake let them, their mother made them clean up and change clothes afterward. Our Lady of the Lake waited up the road with its doors open and its air-conditioning too cold.

Scott walked ahead of the other two with a paper grocery sack folded under his arm. Brian carried a bigger sack. Matt dragged his feet until he saw the first shiny thing in the reeds, then he moved like it was treasure.

The shoreline smelled like wet algae and stale beer. Some cans still had foam dried to the rim. Some were crushed flat, sharp-edged, and cut their fingers if you grabbed wrong.

Scott learned to pinch the can at the bottom, not the top.

Mosquitoes found them anyway.

They worked the coves where people had tied up overnight, the quiet water near docks where the waves pushed trash gently into corners. The sun rose and turned the aluminum bright enough to sting your eyes.

Matt made it a game at first. "I got one," he said, holding it up like a fish.

"Put it in the bag," Brian said.

Matt said, "I know," but he waited an extra second, letting the can gleam.

Scott listened to the cans in the sack as they dropped in—thin metallic clanks, hollow and quick. Each one was five cents. He kept the number in his head and tried not to picture who'd held it last.

Brian found a cluster of cans caught under a low branch and waded in up to his calves without taking his shoes off. Water went dark around his legs. The mud sucked at his soles.

"Don't," Scott started.

Brian didn't look back. He reached deeper, arm disappearing into reeds, and pulled out three cans at once, dripping.

He tossed them into the sack and kept moving like his legs weren't wet.

Matt watched him and then stepped in too, copying, and immediately yelped when something brushed his ankle.

He jumped back onto the rocks, heart in his throat. "Something touched me."

"It's weeds," Brian said.

Scott didn't say anything. He looked down into the water anyway, scanning for shape, for movement, for anything that didn't belong.

They didn't find anything.

They kept going.

By the time the sun was fully up, the sacks were heavy enough to stretch their arms. The metal smell stayed on their hands no matter how they wiped them on their shorts.

Matt started counting out loud. "One, two, three—"

"Stop," Brian said.

Matt stopped, offended. "Why?"

Brian glanced toward the nearest dock where a man sat in a lawn chair with a beer in his hand even though it was still morning. The man watched them without moving his face.

Brian lowered his voice. "Just stop."

Scott understood. He kept his mouth shut and counted in his head instead.

* * *

Scott took the cans to the store in town with their mother because that's where you got paid.

By then, the Corvette was back in St. Louis with their dad. He'd gone home for work after the first weekend and came down again in the station wagon, the back full of groceries and towels and whatever he thought a family needed.

Their mother drove them in the station wagon when she went for groceries. She didn't ask where the cans came from. She didn't say good job. She only said, "Don't spill them in the back," like the worst thing would be mess.

The sacks sat in the cargo area, aluminum shifting with every turn. The smell filled the car.

Matt rolled the window down and stuck his face into the wind.

At the store, Scott carried his sack in both hands and felt the handles bite his fingers. Brian took the bigger sack as if it didn't weigh anything. Matt carried nothing and tried to look like he was helping by holding the door.

Inside, the air was cold and smelled like bread and floor cleaner. People glanced at the sacks and then looked away.

The clerk at the counter wore a cigarette behind his ear. He pulled the first sack open and started counting cans one by one, setting them into a wooden crate with practiced hands.

Scott watched his fingers.

The clerk didn't hurry. He didn't need to. Scott could feel the line forming behind them, the weight of people waiting with milk and cigarettes and fishing licenses.

Matt shifted from foot to foot. "How much we get?"

The clerk looked at him like he was a bug that had learned to talk. "Five cents," he said flatly, and kept counting.

Matt flushed and shut his mouth.

Halfway through the second sack, Scott realized the clerk had miscounted.

Not by much. One can. But one can meant a nickel, and a nickel meant a sparkler later, a candy bar, a soda bottle cold enough to hurt your teeth.

He opened his mouth and felt the words stick.

Brian stood still beside him, face blank, looking past the counter at nothing.

Scott said, softly, "I think that was one more."

The clerk paused.

He stared at Scott a long moment, cigarette still behind his ear, and Scott felt his neck go hot.

Then the clerk reached into the crate and pulled one can out, not even glancing down. He tossed it back into the sack as if it didn't matter.

"There," he said.

Scott's gut clenched. He didn't feel proud. He felt noticed.

A woman behind them laughed under her breath. "Little businessmen," she said to no one, voice light like she meant it as a joke.

Scott didn't turn around.

The clerk finished counting and slid a handful of coins across the counter. Brian scooped them up and dropped them into his pocket without counting in front of anyone.

Outside, the sun hit them hard and the air felt thick again. Brian said, "We got it," like it was a job completed.

Matt reached for the coins in Brian's pocket. "Let me see."

Brian slapped his hand away without looking. "Not here."

Matt glared and then jogged ahead, kicking at gravel like it was the road's fault.

The fireworks store sat next door with its windows full of color.

Scott saw it first. Red and gold boxes stacked behind glass, Black Cat bricks with the cat's face grinning, bottle rockets fanned out like feathers. A hand-lettered sign said SNAKES 10¢ and PUNKS 5¢ FOR 3.

Brian stopped walking.

Their mother was still inside the grocery, talking to someone near the register. Through the window Scott could see her nodding, not looking toward the door.

"How much do we have?" Matt asked.

Brian pulled the coins from his pocket and counted without showing anyone. His lips moved. Then he looked at the fireworks store and back at the grocery.

"Enough," he said.

The bell on the door rang when they went in. The man behind the counter had a mustache and a cigarette that he didn't take out of his mouth when he talked.

"You boys need help?"

Brian pointed at the Black Cats. "One brick."

The man reached up without checking the price. He set the brick on the counter and waited.

"Bottle rockets," Scott said. "The ones with the sticks."

"How many?"

Scott looked at Brian. Brian held up two fingers.

"Two packs," the man said, and set them down.

Matt pressed his face close to the glass case where the snakes sat in their little boxes. "Those," he said. "The black ones."

"Snakes." The man pulled out a box and added it to the pile. "Anything else?"

Brian looked at what they had. Then he said, "Punks."

The man dropped a bundle of brown sticks on the counter, tied with a rubber band. "That's two-forty even."

Brian counted out the coins one at a time. The man watched his fingers and didn't say anything about the smell.

Outside, Scott carried the bag against his chest. It was lighter than the cans had been but felt heavier.

Their mother came out of the grocery with two paper sacks and didn't ask what they were holding.

Scott walked behind his brothers and watched her load everything into the car. She moved with the same efficiency she used at the cabin—bags placed, trunk shut, keys ready.

She didn't ask what the store clerk had said.

She didn't ask if anyone had been rude.

She only said, "Wash your hands when we get back."

* * *

That night, the Harrises came by for their parents.

Mrs. Harris stood on the porch in a yellow dress and laughed at something their father said. Mr. Harris waited by the car with his hands in his pockets, patient the way some men were patient when their wives talked too long.

"We'll be back by ten," their mother said. "Maybe eleven."

She looked at Brian when she said it. Brian nodded once.

"There's sandwich stuff in the fridge. Don't go in the water."

Then they were gone, taillights through the trees, and the cabin got quiet in a way it only got quiet when no adults were in it.

Matt said, "Now?"

Brian looked out the screen door at the cove. The sun was down but the sky still held light at the edges. Across the water, someone else's dock had people on it—teenagers, maybe, shapes moving in the dusk.

"Now," Brian said.

They took the bag down to the seawall. The rocks were still warm from the day. An empty soda bottle sat wedged between two stones where someone had left it. Scott found a flat spot and set out the Black Cats in a row while Brian unwrapped the bottle rockets.

Matt opened the snakes and lined up the little black pellets on a piece of slate. "You light them and they grow," he said, like he was explaining it to someone who didn't know.

"I know," Scott said.

Brian handed out punks. They were rough and fibrous, like incense sticks that hadn't been dipped right. He struck a match and lit the end of his, and the tip glowed orange and started to smoke.

Scott lit his own and watched the ember climb.

The first Black Cat went off too fast—Scott lit the fuse and it cracked before he could step back. His ears rang. Matt laughed and covered his mouth.

Brian set a bottle rocket in an empty soda bottle and angled it toward the water. The fuse caught, hissed, and then the rocket screamed up and out over the cove, a red streak that popped somewhere above the middle.

From across the water, someone whooped.

Then a bottle rocket came back.

It arced high and wide, trailing sparks, and hit the water twenty feet from their dock with a small splash and a muffled crack.

Matt said, "They're shooting at us."

Brian was already loading another rocket. "Get more," he said.

Scott grabbed two from the pack and handed one to Matt. His fingers were shaking but not from cold. The punk's ember touched the fuse and the paper caught and hissed and he barely got his hand clear before it launched.

The rocket went sideways, curving wrong, and fizzled out before it reached the other shore.

Another one came back, closer this time. It hit the rocks behind them and the report echoed off the bluff.

Brian fired again. Matt fired. Scott loaded and fired and loaded again. The smoke rose around them in thin ribbons and the smell got into everything—sulfur and paper and something sharper underneath.

Across the cove, the teenagers were laughing. Scott couldn't see their faces, just shapes moving, and the small orange points of their own punks.

He didn't know how long it lasted. The bottle rockets ran out first, and then the Black Cats, and then they were down to the snakes and nobody wanted to waste those on a war.

Brian held up his hands in the dark, palms out, like a signal. Across the water, someone did the same.

The last rocket from the other side went straight up instead of toward them. It burst red and fell in pieces toward the water.

Matt said, "Did we win?"

Nobody answered.

Scott lit one of the snakes on the flat rock and watched it swell and twist, black ash rising into a shape that looked like nothing and everything. The sizzle was quieter than the rockets. The smoke smelled different—chalky, almost sweet.

When it stopped growing, it just sat there, curled and spent.

They walked back up to the cabin without talking. The screen door slapped behind them. Brian checked the lock on the back door even though their parents weren't home to notice.

Scott washed his hands in the kitchen sink and the water ran gray. The smell stayed anyway.

He lay in the room he shared with his brothers and listened to the cove go quiet. No more rockets. No more laughter from across the water. Just the dock tapping the way it always did, and the ceiling fan clicking once per turn.

His fingers still smelled like smoke.

He didn't know if they'd won or lost or if it mattered. He only knew the bag was empty now, and the money was gone, and tomorrow the cans would be back in the reeds where people left them.

He closed his eyes and let the tapping carry him under.

CH 08

The Quiet Man

ONE MORNING, the grandfather's boat made a different sound than their father's.
Not louder. Just older. Wood creak underfoot. A slow knock where the bow touched a small wave. The motor idled like it was thinking.

Brian sat on the bench seat with his knees apart and his hands on the tackle box, waiting to be told what to do. Scott sat still and watched the shoreline slide by. Matt kept leaning over the side until Brian pressed him back with a forearm.

"Sit," the grandfather said.

Matt sat.

They were in a quiet cove where the water lay flat and green. You could hear insects and the distant rise and fall of a boat engine from the channel, but out here it sounded like it belonged to someone else.

The grandfather cut the motor and let them drift.

The sudden quiet made Brian's ears ring.

The grandfather opened the tackle box and moved through it with hands that didn't hesitate. He didn't explain. He pulled out hooks and split shot and a small dull knife with a worn handle.

"You," he said to Brian, and nodded at the line spool.

Brian grabbed it fast. Too fast. The line uncoiled and looped across his fingers.

The grandfather didn't look up. He only said, "Easy."

Brian forced his hands to slow. He fed the line out again, controlled this time, feeling it slide cool and smooth across his skin.

The grandfather held a hook up between thumb and forefinger. "Watch," he said.

Brian leaned in, eyes narrowing.

The grandfather's fingers moved. Around. Through. Tightened. A knot that appeared without effort. He tugged it once, hard, and the line held.

Brian nodded like he understood.

"You do," the grandfather said.

Brian swallowed and took the hook. The barb caught the pad of his thumb lightly and he flinched.

The grandfather's eyes flicked to his hand. "Don't fight it," he said, and went back to the tackle box.

Brian threaded the line the way he'd just watched. It didn't go clean. The hook spun. The line slipped. His fingers started to sweat.

Matt made a small impatient sound. "Come on."

Brian ignored him and tried again. He could feel the grandfather's presence behind him without looking.

When he pulled the knot tight, it cinched wrong. The line kinked.

He started to undo it.

The grandfather reached over and put a hand on Brian's wrist, not stopping him, just anchoring.

"If you pull," the grandfather said, voice low, "it bites."

Brian went still.

The grandfather slid his hand away. He didn't fix the knot. He let Brian do it.

Brian breathed out slowly and eased the line loose with small careful movements until the kink freed. He retied it, slower, feeling the line drag against his skin, watching the hook like it could jump.

This time the knot sat neat.

He tugged it once.

It held.

The grandfather nodded once, as if that was all he'd been waiting for. He handed Brian a sinker and then the knife.

The knife handle was warm from the grandfather's pocket.

Brian held it like a grown-up, too tight.

"Not like that," the grandfather said.

Brian adjusted his grip without asking how.

The grandfather pointed at the bait—worms in a damp tin, dirt clinging to them.

Brian felt the familiar twist of disgust in his stomach and pushed it down. He pinched a worm and tried not to think about it being alive.

The worm slid, slick.

He tightened his fingers and felt it give.

Matt laughed. "You killed it."

Brian's face burned.

"It's fine," the grandfather said, and his voice made it true.

Brian threaded the worm onto the hook, hands steadying as he did. The hook point pricked his nail once and he stopped moving immediately, breath held.

The grandfather watched him and said nothing.

Brian waited until the hook stopped moving in his hand, until his fingers stopped shaking, until he could feel his own heartbeat slow.

Then he finished.

* * *

When it was time to cast, Brian stood up too fast and the boat rocked.

Matt grabbed the seat edge with both hands. Scott's shoulder hit the side. Water slapped the hull once, sharp.

The grandfather didn't raise his voice. He just looked at Brian.

Brian froze, rod halfway lifted.

"Sit," the grandfather said.

Brian sat. The bench felt suddenly too small.

The grandfather pointed toward the water. "Wait," he said.

Brian stared at the surface. It looked empty. It wasn't empty. He knew that. He could feel the fish down there the way he could feel storms before anyone named them.

The grandfather held his own rod loosely. The line ran straight down into the green.

For a while, nothing happened.

Matt started to fidget. Scott stayed still.

Brian wanted to do something. Reel. Adjust. Prove he was paying attention. He watched the tip of the rod like it might tell him a secret.

The grandfather's line twitched once, small.

The grandfather didn't move.

It twitched again.

Brian sucked in a breath and started to reach for the handle, as if helping.

The grandfather lifted one finger, not looking at him.

Brian stopped.

The line tightened slowly, the bend in the rod deepening like the fish was thinking.

"Now," the grandfather said, barely above the water's sound.

He lifted the rod in one smooth motion and reeled with steady turns. No jerking. No speed. The fish came up in silver flashes, resisting, then yielding, then resisting again.

Brian watched the grandfather's hands and felt his own hands itching to copy.

When the fish broke the surface, it slapped and spun, water spraying cold on their legs.

Matt squealed.

Brian leaned forward automatically.

"Don't," the grandfather said, and the word stopped him again.

The fish thrashed harder, hook glinting. Brian saw the barb and pictured it in skin. His skin tightened. He didn't know where.

The grandfather waited.

The fish tired itself in quick bursts, each one smaller than the last. The boat settled. The water smoothed.

Only then did the grandfather reach down and take the line above the hook with two fingers, calm as if he'd done it a thousand times.

He lifted the fish into the boat and laid it in the bottom, where it flopped twice and then went still.

Brian stared at it, chest tight.

The grandfather unhooked it with a quick twist of the wrist and dropped it into the livewell.

He handed the rod to Brian.

The handle felt different in Brian's hands now. He held it with less force, like squeezing didn't make anything happen faster.

The grandfather nodded toward the water again. "Wait," he said.

Brian looked out at the green surface and kept his mouth shut.

The cove held its quiet.

*　*　*

When the grandfather finally started the motor again, it caught on the second pull and settled into a low steady thrum.

They rode back slower than Scott expected. Not because the boat couldn't go faster. Because the grandfather didn't hurry things once they were underway. The shoreline slid by in long pieces—oak and hickory, a stand of walnut, a fallen tree half in the water with roots exposed like fingers. The sun climbed higher and the channel noise grew louder in the distance, but out in their quiet cove it stayed muted.

Matt leaned against the seat and let his eyes droop as if he might fall asleep. Brian kept watching the water, still locked on the idea that something would happen again if he paid attention hard enough. Scott watched the grandfather's hands on the tiller, relaxed and sure.

At the dock, the grandfather cut the motor and let the boat drift in. He didn't bump the boards. He didn't rush the tie-up. He stepped out, tied one knot, then another, each one clean.

Rick stood on the porch when they came up the steps, coffee in his hand, watching like he'd been waiting. His eyes went to the livewell first.

"Catch anything?" he asked, voice casual.

The grandfather nodded once. "A few," he said.

Rick stepped down onto the dock and lifted the livewell lid, peering in. The fish flashed silver, trapped in a shallow dark space.

Matt leaned over eagerly. "I want to see," he said.

Rick closed the lid too quickly, and Matt's hand got caught between plastic and wood. Matt yelped and pulled back, more surprised than hurt.

Rick said, "Watch it," too sharp.

The grandfather looked at Rick, then at Matt's hand, then away. He didn't scold Rick. He didn't soften the moment either.

He said, "Get the knife," to Brian.

Brian ran inside and came back with the worn knife, handle warm from earlier. He held it out like a tool that could change everything.

The grandfather took it and moved to the cleaning board Rick kept by the water—old wood, stained dark, grooves cut into it from years of use.

Matt edged closer, curious again. Scott stayed a half-step back, already feeling where the day could turn.

Brian stood nearest, breathing shallowly.

The grandfather lifted the livewell lid and reached in without flinching. He grasped a fish behind the head and pulled it out. It thrashed once in his hand, then calmed under firm grip.

Brian watched the fish's mouth open and close.

Matt whispered, "Is it dead?"

The grandfather said, "Not yet," as if the answer wasn't a warning.

Rick shifted his coffee mug from one hand to the other. "We keeping 'em?" he asked.

The grandfather nodded once. "We'll fry 'em," he said.

Matt smiled. He liked the simplicity of an outcome.

Scott watched Brian's face. Brian wasn't smiling.

The grandfather set the fish on the board. Its tail slapped once, wet and quick.

Brian flinched.

The grandfather's knife moved.

Not fast. Not showy. Just work—one cut, then another. A twist of the wrist. The fish stopped fighting. The dock kept tapping under them like it always did.

Matt stared hard, mouth open slightly. Scott looked away once, then forced himself to look back. Brian stared at the grandfather's hands as if memorizing how a person could do that without changing expression.

Rick said, "You got it," as if encouraging the grandfather.

The grandfather didn't look up.

He cleaned the fish, slid the meat into a pan, and pushed the rest aside with the back of the blade. He rinsed the board with a bucket of lake water. He wiped the knife on his jeans and handed it back to Brian, handle first.

Brian took it carefully, like it could bite.

The grandfather said, "Put it away."

Brian nodded and went inside.

Scott stayed on the dock with Matt while the adults moved into the cabin, the sound of pans and water and their mother's voice rising for a moment, then dropping again.

Matt said, "That was cool."

Scott didn't answer.

Matt nudged him with an elbow. "Did you see how he did it? Like nothing."

Scott looked down at the wet boards. He could still see the fish's tail in his mind, the sudden slap.

He said, "He always does that," and the sentence wasn't admiration or disgust. It was just fact.

Matt leaned over the edge of the dock and watched the water. "I want to be good at stuff," he said, and Scott heard how young it sounded.

Scott looked at his brother, surprised by the honesty.

Before he could answer, Brian came back out and sat on the porch steps, elbows on his knees.

He held a piece of fishing line in his hands.

He was tying the knot again.

His fingers moved slower this time. More patient. He pulled the loop tight and then loosened it gently, checking it, feeling for the bite the grandfather had warned about.

Scott watched him do it and felt something settle in him—the rare sense that Brian could learn a thing without turning it into a competition.

Brian didn't look up.

He tied the knot again anyway, as if the repetition itself was the lesson.

CH 09

Red Feather

IN THE MORNING, Scott heard the cardinal before he saw it. The call came sharp through the screens: two notes, a pause, two more. Insistent, like a knock you couldn't ignore. Scott stood at the kitchen sink with his hands under running water, rinsing a coffee mug that didn't need rinsing, and listened until the sound started to feel like pressure.

He dried his hands on the dish towel and stepped onto the porch.

The air was already warm. The lake smell rose from the cove—gasoline, algae, sun on boards. Somewhere down the channel, a boat engine rose and fell and then faded.

On the oak by the porch steps, the cardinal sat bright as a warning. Red against green. It cocked its head and called again, not afraid of the cabin or the people inside it.

Scott watched the bird hop along the branch, claws sure on bark. He felt the small, ridiculous urge to throw something at it just to make it move. To prove he could change a thing.

From inside, he heard Linda's voice say, "Shoes," the same correction she always made. He heard Brian moving in the kitchen, drawers opening and closing. He heard Matt's bare feet slap once on the boards and then stop.

The cardinal called again.

Scott stood still on the porch boards and felt the old day rise in him without invitation—the heat, the climb, the rubber snap.

He didn't know why the memory came now. He only knew it came with the same bodily certainty as the smell of wet wood after a storm.

He watched the bird for a long moment, then looked away first, as if not looking was a kind of mercy.

* * *

Later that week, the slingshots were warm from their pockets.

They'd climbed higher than they usually did, past the place where the dirt thinned and the limestone showed through like bone. From up there, you could see the lake in pieces—bright through leaves, flat and distant—and the cabin roof looked small enough to pick up.

The cardinal was loud before they saw it.

It flashed red against the green, hopping along a branch near the top of an oak, head cocked, calling like it was arguing with the air. It didn't seem afraid.

Matt spotted it first. "Look," he whispered, already pointing.

Brian shaded his eyes. "That's high."

Scott didn't say anything at first. He tracked the distance and the branches in the way. He could feel the trouble in it, the way you could feel a rock shifting under your shoe before it slid.

Matt pulled his slingshot out and gave it a little shake, like that helped. "Bet I can hit it."

"You won't," Brian said automatically. "That's too far."

Matt stretched the rubber anyway, testing it, feeling the give. He wanted them watching. That was the point.

Scott cleared his throat. "It's a cardinal."

Matt frowned. "So?"

"You're not supposed to shoot them."

"Why not?"

Scott hesitated. He didn't have a reason that would work. He only had the feeling in his gut.

Brian snorted. "They're birds."

The cardinal hopped again, higher, as if it was climbing out of reach.

Matt reached into his pocket and pulled out a smooth stone he'd been carrying all morning, one he'd already chosen for something. He set it in the leather pouch and pulled the band back.

"Don't," Scott said, too quiet.

Matt's arm shook a little—not from the weight, but from the stretch. He lined it up the way Brian had shown him once, elbow locked, eye squinted.

Scott looked at Brian.

Brian didn't stop him.

The stone snapped forward with a dry, sharp sound. The rubber slapped the frame. For a half-second nothing happened, and then the bird dropped.

It didn't fall straight. It clipped a branch, then another. Feathers burst loose like red scraps. It hit the ground somewhere below them with a sound that was more felt than heard.

No one said anything.

Matt's arm was still raised. He lowered it slowly.

"I hit it," he said. His voice wasn't proud. It was surprised.

Scott was already moving.

* * *

The three of them climbed down in silence, sliding on loose dirt, grabbing branches too thin to trust. The ground smelled damp and sharp where the bird had landed.

It lay on its side near the base of the tree, wings half-open, one eye closed. Its chest moved. Once. Then again, smaller.

Matt crouched. "It's just stunned."

Brian nodded quickly. "Yeah. Birds do that."

Scott stayed standing, hands clenched at his sides. The red looked wrong up close. Too bright. Like something meant to be seen from far away, not held in your eyes at this distance.

The bird fluttered once, weakly, and made a sound that wasn't a call. Just breath.

Matt reached out, then stopped. "Should I...?"

Brian shook his head. "Don't touch it. You'll scare it."

They waited.

The bird didn't get up.

Scott felt time stretch. He could hear the cicadas again, loud and normal, as if the woods had already moved on.

Matt picked up his slingshot and slipped it back into his pocket. The rubber snapped softly against the metal frame.

"It'll be fine," he said, like he was saying it to himself.

Brian said, "Yeah," too fast.

Scott didn't say anything.

They left the bird there, under the tree, red against brown leaves, and walked back toward the bikes without looking behind them.

* * *

At the cabin, Matt couldn't hold it in.

He started talking before his bike was even leaned against the porch rail. "We saw this cardinal up high and I—"

Their mother glanced out the screen door. "What?" she called.

"Nothing," Brian said, and his tone shut the air down.

Matt swallowed the rest, face hot, and waited until they were out of her sightline.

Near the steps, he tried again, smaller. "I hit it."

Brian shook his head once. "You almost hit it."

Matt stared at him. "I did."

"It was too high," Brian said, like that settled it. "You didn't. You almost did."

Matt opened his mouth, then shut it.

Scott stood beside them with his hands on the porch rail, fingers wrapped tight around the warm wood. He could feel the bird's small chest moving under his eyes, the way it had gotten smaller.

Their father's voice came from inside the cabin, talking about something that needed fixing. A drawer slid. Metal clinked.

Matt said, "Yeah," finally, and the word sounded like he'd swallowed it.

Brian nodded once, satisfied.

Scott didn't correct them.

He went to the back room and washed his hands longer than he needed to, water cold over his knuckles, as if scrubbing could change what had happened in the woods.

CH 10

In the Channel

BRIAN STOOD at the end of the dock and watched the channel like he was waiting for something to break the surface.
Behind him, Jake's feet slapped the boards, quick and impatient, then went still.

The water was smooth enough to carry reflections, then a boat passed and cut it into pieces. A wake rolled into the cove and made the dock lift and settle, lift and settle, the rope creaking once where it rubbed the cleat.

Out in the open water, something long and pale rose and slapped back down with a sound like wet wood. A second later the surface closed over as if it had never happened.

Brian kept looking anyway.

A few mornings later, Uncle Carl ran early, the way he always insisted on.

The main channel lay wide and empty. Mist lifted off the water in low sheets that parted as the boat slid through. The engine sat low, a controlled sound that didn't bounce off the bluffs yet.

Brian sat where he'd been told. Up front, knees braced, one hand on the console. Scott sat behind him, eyes moving constantly. Matt tucked between seats, legs drawn up, fingers trailing the cold edge of fiberglass until Brian tapped his wrist once to make him stop.

Uncle Carl didn't talk much when he drove.

He kept his eyes on the surface like it might give him a sign. The sunlight hadn't reached the channel yet. The air was cool enough to raise goosebumps on Brian's arms.

"This is spoonbill water," Uncle Carl said finally, without turning his head. "They jump this time of morning."

Matt leaned forward. "What makes 'em jump?"

Uncle Carl shrugged. "Nobody knows."

Brian stared at the water ahead and tried to imagine something big enough to matter out there, under the green.

They saw the shadow before they saw the fish.

A long dark shape surged up ahead of them, moving too fast to make sense at first. Then it broke the surface entirely.

The spoonbill launched clear of the water.

For a half second it hung there, pale underneath, heavy as a log, its long flat bill out in front of it. Then the body rolled in the air, wrong in its arc, and Brian understood it was coming straight at them.

The impact hit like someone dropping wood onto the deck.

The hull shuddered. Water exploded up and cold spray slapped Brian's face. The fish landed half in the boat, half against the side, and thrashed instantly—tail beating the deck, body too big and too alive for the space it had fallen into.

Matt screamed and tried to scramble backward. His foot slipped on wet fiberglass and he caught himself on the seat edge, eyes wide.

Scott froze with his hands raised, as if holding still could keep the fish from touching him.

Brian lunged forward without thinking, then stopped short as the tail whipped past where his legs had been.

"DON'T TOUCH IT," Uncle Carl shouted.

He cut the engine in one clean motion.

The sudden quiet felt worse than the noise.

The spoonbill bucked and writhed. Its bill scraped across fiberglass with a hollow, bone-on-plastic sound. Each strike rattled the boat. Water and slime smeared the deck. The fish's body flexed hard enough that Brian could see the muscle through slick skin.

"Everybody still," Uncle Carl said, voice sharp and controlled. "You hear me? Still."

Brian pressed his back against the console and forced his hands open. His fingers wanted to grab something. There was nothing safe to grab.

The tail struck again. It missed Matt by inches and slapped the bench with a wet crack.

Matt made a small sound like he was trying not to cry.

Uncle Carl dropped low and planted his feet wide, balanced. He grabbed the net—not to catch the fish, but to guide it. He held the rim between the boys and the thrashing body like a shield, nudging the fish toward the side each time it surged.

"Easy," Uncle Carl said, not to the boys, not to the fish. Just to the moment. "Easy now."

The fish found the gunwale.

It heaved once, tail slapping hard enough to rock the boat. It slid, belly scraping, and then it was gone—back into the channel with a violent splash that sent cold water over the side and into the boat.

The ripples widened. The mist closed over the surface again as if nothing had happened.

No one moved.

Uncle Carl exhaled once, loud. "That's why you don't reach for things you don't understand," he said.

Matt let out a laugh that was too high and too loud. His hands shook when he wiped water off his face.

Scott stared at the water and didn't blink.

Brian looked down at the deck where the fish had been. The fiberglass was scuffed. A wet smear shone in the low light. His knees trembled without him meaning them to.

Uncle Carl restarted the engine. It settled back into its steady hum.

"Sit down," Uncle Carl said, like they'd been standing up doing something wrong. "All of you."

They did.

They ran on down the channel, the sun starting to burn through the fog in thin stripes.

No one spoke again for a while.

***

Back at the dock, Uncle Carl tied the boat off and stepped out first.

"Get the bucket," he said.

Brian grabbed it without asking which one. He filled it from the lake and carried it back, water sloshing against his shins. The metal handle cut into his palm.

Uncle Carl took the bucket and dumped it over the deck. Water rolled across the scuffed fiberglass and over the side in sheets, carrying slime and bits of grass with it.

"Do it again," Uncle Carl said.

Brian did.

Matt hovered at the edge of the dock, still wet, arms wrapped around himself. Scott knelt and stared at the scuff marks like they were handwriting.

"You all right?" Uncle Carl asked without looking up.

Brian opened his mouth and felt words fail him. Fine. Good. Huge. He chose the one that ended the question fastest.

"Yeah," he said.

Uncle Carl nodded once, satisfied, and went back to rinsing the deck, as if the morning could be washed down to a clean surface.

Brian poured the last bucket and watched the water run off. The scuff stayed.

He set the bucket down carefully so it wouldn't clang and draw attention.

Then he wiped his hands on his shorts and stood still until his legs stopped shaking.

Part Two

CH 11

The Resort Lights

WHEN SCOTT WAS twelve, the boats were so close together their music overlapped.
You could hear three songs at once and none of them all the way through. Somebody laughed hard, too loud, like he was trying to prove he was having fun. A woman somewhere kept saying, "Hold my beer," and then giggling before anyone could answer.

They'd eaten early on the water before coming here.

Ozark Bar-B-Que sat loud and bright on its docks, boats tied up in a line like it was a marina and not a restaurant. Engines idled and made the boards vibrate. The air inside had been warm and sticky, smoke and sauce in everything. Long picnic tables ran lengthwise, scarred and shiny where hands had rubbed them smooth. Paper napkins in metal dispensers that didn't do much.

Matt had begged for chocolate cream pie until their mother said yes without looking up.

At the next table, two men talked over each other with beer bottles sweating on the wood. One of them laughed too hard and then lowered his voice and didn't lower it enough.

"You stay wide of that reef over there," he said. "People cut inside like it's a shortcut and then you're dead in the water."

Reef belonged to oceans. Not here.

Scott didn't ask what it meant. He watched Brian's attention shift, quick, as if the word had been added to a list in his head.

Outside again, the dock boards had been hot under their feet. Their father had untied the boat and pushed them off clean. The channel opened ahead, bright and busy.

By the time they reached Four Seasons, dusk was coming on and the lake looked dressed up—more boats than usual, more lights, music spilling across the water in thin overlapping pieces.

Their boat rocked in place, tied off with a rope his father had double-checked twice. The rope stayed
 tight. The knot looked neat. The lake still moved underneath it anyway.

The Glastron sat low in the water, fifteen feet of fiberglass with the big Evinrude on the back. Fast, their father said. Too fast for how light it was, their mother said. The same boat from that James Bond movie—Scott had heard that a dozen times. Right now it looked small against the cruisers tied up nearby, their wakes already making it bob.

"Don't lean," his mother said, not looking at him. She had her hand on Matt's shoulder like she could feel the whole water through him.

"I'm not," he said, even though he was.

His brothers were in front of him on the bow. Brian kept shifting his feet, testing the boards of the deck the way he did on docks. Scott sat low, arms around his knees, watching other boats more than the sky.

The fireworks started late.

At first it was just a thin whistle and then a bloom of light that made faces change. The lake turned red, then green, then white. A hundred boats flashed and went dark and flashed again. People shouted each time something burst, like the sound could push the light higher

Scott forgot to breathe.

When the big ones went off, the sound hit his chest and made it feel hollow for a second. He laughed without meaning to. His mother squeezed his shoulder once, the way she did when she wanted him to settle.

"Look," Matt whispered, pointing at a shape in the sky that fell in silver threads, slow and beautiful.

His father didn't look up right away. He kept his eyes on the water, the way he always did when they were on the boat, as if the lake had rules you could only see if you stared hard enough. When he finally glanced up, it was quick, like checking a clock.

Across the water, a man stood on the back of a bigger boat and waved a lit cigarette around as he talked. The ember drew bright circles in the dark. Someone else clapped him on the shoulder too hard and the cigarette ash fell in a small glowing line onto the deck.

His mother's lips tightened. She didn't say anything.

The last fireworks were the loudest. They came so fast the sky didn't have time to go dark between them. The lake looked like daylight for seconds at a time. Then it went black again.

When it ended, there was a pause.

The silence lasted just long enough to feel wrong.

Then engines started.

Not one. Not two. Everywhere.

The lake filled with the sound of motors being pushed hard, the low growl turning into a higher whine as people throttled up without easing into it. Navigation lights snapped on in scattered places—red, green, small white bulbs bobbing on dark water like Christmas ornaments someone had thrown away.

"Stay seated," his father said.

He didn't raise his voice. He didn't have to. The sound around them made everything feel like shouting anyway.

His mother leaned toward him. "Feet under you," she said. "Hold the rail."

He slid his feet back and grabbed the side of the boat, fingers wrapping around cold metal.

Their boat pulled away from the tied line and angled out into the channel. Scott turned to look behind them once, then faced forward again, eyes wide but steady. Brian stood by the console, one hand on the windshield frame, watching the water ahead like he could read it.

The first wake hit them broadside.

It wasn't a ripple. It wasn't even a wave the way he understood waves. It was a moving wall, dark and heavy, rising up out of nothing. The boat lifted hard, one side higher than the other. His stomach jumped and then dropped.

His mother's hand tightened on his arm. "Hold," she said.

The boat slammed down. Water sprayed up, cold against his face, and he tasted gas and lake and something metallic.

Ahead of them, another boat cut across the channel too fast, its bow high. The man driving it stood up like he was proud of himself. Someone on the back raised both arms in the air and whooped.

His father didn't say anything. His jaw worked once.

Off to their right, closer to the lodge side of the channel, someone shouted, "Stay wide!"

The next wake hit and lifted them again, and Scott couldn't tell who the warning was for until he heard the word that followed.

"Reef!" the voice yelled. "Stay wide of the reef!"

His father's shoulders tightened. He didn't argue with a rule like that. He eased their bow farther out into the channel, away from the shoreline he couldn't see cleanly in the dark.

Ahead, a boat's engine pitch changed suddenly—high to low in an instant—then there was a hard jolt that made its bow drop. The boat stopped as if it had hit something solid, and then began to drift sideways in the stacked wakes.

Lights swung. People stood up and waved arms. Another boat swerved too late and missed it by a few feet, throwing a wake that made the stopped boat rock.

His father didn't shout. He only held the wheel steady and let faster boats make their own bad decisions around them.

They moved forward into the channel with the rest of the boats, and the wakes stacked on top of each other. Every time the boat rose, he couldn't see anything but black sky. Every time it dropped, the water disappeared beneath them like it had been pulled away.

Brian swore once. Not loud. Just a small word that meant he was scared.

The lights on other boats blurred and jerked and jumped as they hit waves. Red and green and white. Close, then far. Here, then gone. The dark made distance feel false.

At one point a boat came up behind them and passed too close, its engine screaming. The wake it threw hit them from the side and then from behind, twisting the boat as it rose. He felt his body slide on the wet seat. His fingers slipped on the rail. His heart hammered, loud enough to drown out the engine.

His mother leaned across him, her forearm pressing his chest back into place. "Don't let go," she said into his ear.

"I'm not," he lied.

The boat hit another wake and pitched up. For a second he saw nothing but the black channel ahead, and then a white light flashed across the water as another boat turned, and he saw how many waves there were. Not one. Not two. A whole field of them, ridges and troughs, moving different directions, crossing and building into peaks that looked taller than they should have been.

He thought of the cabin roof. The way it sat low under the trees.

These felt higher.

Scott started counting under his breath. He didn't know what the numbers meant. He only knew the sound of it made him feel less alone.

Brian didn't count. He watched. His body leaned and corrected with the boat, like he was trying to become part of it.

His father held the wheel steady and kept them pointed into the worst of it. He didn't try to dodge. There was nowhere to dodge to.

Somewhere out in the dark someone shouted, "Slow down!" The words got eaten by engines and spray.

His mother whispered something he couldn't hear. Maybe a prayer. Maybe a list. Maybe nothing at all.

When they finally reached the cove, the water changed.

The waves didn't stop, not right away, but they softened, the peaks losing their edges. The shoreline closed in. The darkness felt less wide. The boat's engine dropped to a lower sound as his father eased back, careful now, like they were sneaking up on something.

His hands hurt from gripping the rail.

He didn't realize he was shaking until his mother put both hands on his shoulders and turned him to face her. Her eyes moved over him fast—face, arms, legs—counting without counting. Then she nodded once, as if the numbers came out right.

They tied up at the dock without talking about what had just happened.

The boards were slick under their shoes. The dock creaked the way it always did. The cabin sat behind the trees with one light on, steady and small.

Inside, later, adults would say things like, "That was a show," and, "Those people are crazy," and then laugh, too high.

He didn't laugh.

He lay in the bed he shared with his brothers and listened to boats moving out on the channel, engines still rising and falling in the distance. In the dark, the mattress shifted each time one of them turned.

No one said a word about the ride home.

He kept seeing the waves lifting them and dropping them, again and again, and the feeling that there had been nothing to hold onto but the rail in his hands.

CH 12

Hold Fast

SCOTT STOOD on the porch with his phone open to the weather, thumb smudging the glass. A notification sat on his screen:

WATCH *until 7:00 PM*

Across the channel, the sky had a green bruise under the gray, and the air went still the way it did right before wind arrived.

Jake and Emily were on the dock anyway, leaning over the water, and Owen filmed the clouds like clouds were content. Scott stepped down one step and said, "Off the dock."

Jake looked back, annoyed. "Why."

Scott held up his phone. "Because a storm's coming," he said. "Lightning hits water. And docks are basically lightning rods."

They didn't like it, but they moved—slow, angry, testing whether he meant it.

Inside, Linda's footsteps kept a measured pace in the kitchen. Rick stood at the window with his hat in his hand, staring out at the channel.

"Wind's picking up," Rick said. Then his brow furrowed. "Where's the boat?"

"Tied up," Scott said.

Rick nodded, satisfied, and went back to counting the water with his eyes.

Scott looked at the green bruise on the horizon and felt the old day rise in him like a reflex.

That afternoon, the sky changed without asking.

One minute it was blue enough to trust—wide, open, harmless—and the boys were stretched out in their usual places, Matt with his feet on the seat, Scott trailing his fingers through the wake, Brian standing near the console like he belonged there. The arm of the lake ran long and quiet ahead of them, trees crowding the water's edge, cicadas loud enough to flatten thought.

Then the color came.

Not gray. Not black. Green, dark and bruised, with a purple seam running low beneath it. It rolled over the treetops ahead of them like something being pulled fast across a table.

Their mother saw it and didn't hesitate.

She swung the wheel hard. The bow cut across the wake, sending spray up and back. "Hold on," she said—not loud, not panicked. A command, nothing more.

The engine rose as she pushed the throttle forward until it stopped. The boat leapt, skimming now, shoreline blurring. Wind came first, sharp and sudden, lifting the surface of the lake into ripples that ran the wrong way.

Matt laughed once, then stopped.

The air thickened. Leaves flew sideways, skittering across the water like thrown things. The sky ahead collapsed inward, the colors folding over each other until there was no blue left at all.

"Life jackets," their mother said.

They moved at once. No arguing. No jokes. Brian helped Matt with the strap, tugging it tight without looking at him. Scott pulled his own on and sat still, eyes fixed on the narrowing water ahead.

The wind hit them broadside. The boat rocked, then steadied as their mother corrected, jaw set, eyes scanning for somewhere—anywhere—to land.

"Millstone," she said, not to them exactly. A destination she could see in her head if not through the rain.

She pushed toward it anyway, but the engine note changed as the bow met shallower water. The boat lost speed and dropped heavy, the wind catching more of it at once. Their mother pulled the throttle back, eyes hard, choosing not to break the lower unit on rock she couldn't see.

The seconds stretched. The shoreline slid by slower than it should have. The sky kept closing in.

Then she swung the wheel toward the nearest cove and took the first dock that offered anything solid.

A dock came into view through the rain, boards pale and slick, a narrow ladder and a metal box bolted to the side of the cabin wall. It wasn't their dock. It didn't matter.

The rain arrived in sheets. The lake went white with it.

She cut the engine near the boards, let momentum carry them. "Now," she said.

They scrambled. Wet planks. Slipping feet. The rope was already lifting, snapping tight as the wind caught the bow and began to pull the boat away from the dock.

Their mother reached for the line, but the wind surged again, stronger, yanking the boat outward. Matt cried out as the hull lurched.

Brian didn't think.

He jumped.

Bare feet hit the dock hard. He slid, caught himself, hands closing around the rope just as it burned through his palms. The boat surged again, pulling him forward, his weight pitched toward the water.

He wrapped the line once around the cleat, then again, faster than he knew how, his arms shaking with the strain. The rope smoked. His teeth clenched. The wind screamed in his ears.

"Let it go!" their mother shouted.

He didn't.

The line caught. The boat slammed back against the dock, hard enough to rattle teeth, but it held.

Their mother was already moving. She grabbed Matt, then Scott, ushering them off the dock and toward the metal box jutting from the wall, bolted deep into it.

"Down," she said.

They crouched behind it, the metal shuddering as the wind tore at it. The world narrowed to noise and pressure and the smell of wet wood and hot motor. Something struck the roof above them and skittered away. Another blow followed, closer this time.

Brian dropped beside them last, breath ragged, hands clenched into fists he didn't look at.

The sound rose and fell, rose again. The lake vanished behind rain. Trees bent until their tops disappeared. The air felt alive, moving around them, testing.

"Stay with me," their mother said. Her arms came around them, pulling them tight. Three bodies pressed into one space, her back curved around them, shielding, counting breaths.

It lasted longer than any of them could measure.

Then, just as suddenly, it didn't.

The wind loosened its grip. The rain thinned. The noise drained away, leaving a hollow quiet that felt false, like the pause before another blow.

They stayed where they were until their mother moved first.

She stood, looked around, counted. All three boys. All there.

The rope was dark and frayed where it had burned. The dock boards gleamed with water. The lake steamed faintly in the sudden light.

No one said anything.

Their mother put her hand on Brian's shoulder, not the burned hands. "We're going home," she said.

When she restarted the engine, it sounded tired.

They pulled away slow at first, easing back into open water. Matt kept looking over his shoulder, like the storm might follow. Scott stared at the surface for debris. Brian sat with his hands in his lap, staring at nothing.

The sky above them was brighter already.

The lake was not.

CH 13

White Hull

ON THE RIDE back after the storm, Brian didn't speak at first. The lake was wrong in small ways—the surface torn instead of smooth, debris riding low and slow, caught in the current. Leaves clung to the water. A cooler bumped past, lid gone, turning once before drifting out of sight.

Their mother kept the speed steady. Not fast. Not cautious either. Her hands were firm on the wheel. She scanned ahead the way she'd taught them to scan when swimming—wide, patient, already counting.

They saw the boat before they understood it.

It was a Chris-Craft cabin cruiser, bigger than anything he'd ever been on, white hull streaked with dark where it had scraped rock. It sat at an angle no boat should sit at, its bow lifted and twisted, stern wedged against limestone, higher than it should be.

The cliff face behind it was scarred. Fresh marks, pale and raw.

Matt leaned forward. "How did it get up there?"

No one answered.

Brian stood, bracing himself against the rail, eyes moving over the wreck the way their grandfather had taught him to look for fish —slow, methodical. The windows were gone. One rail bent clean back on itself. The canvas top shredded into ribbons that fluttered weakly.

He listened.

He didn't know what he was listening for, only that silence wasn't enough. He strained for voices, for coughing, for anything that would give them a job to do.

Their mother eased the throttle back. The engine dropped to a low murmur. "Is anyone there?" she called, her voice carrying farther than she expected.

Nothing answered.

They drifted closer, careful of what might still be loose. A life jacket floated free near the stern, straps tangled, bright against the water. Matt reached for it and stopped when their mother shook her head.

"Don't," she said. Not sharply. Just enough.

Brian pointed. "There," he said. "Behind the cabin."

They all looked.

There was nothing there. Just shadow and rock and water moving the way water always moved.

They waited longer than made sense.

He counted under his breath—not numbers, just time, marking it the way he always did when he didn't know what else to do. He thought of the cave, of holding still in the dark and listening for breath.

Still nothing.

"We should check," Matt said. He was already half-standing.

Their mother put a hand on his shoulder. "There's nothing we can do," she said. She said it gently, but it landed hard.

They circled once, slow. The boat creaked softly where it pressed against the cliff, a sound like something settling into place.

Brian memorized the angle of the hull. He memorized the silence. Matt memorized the life jacket.

When they pulled away, no one argued.

* * *

The channel between there and home felt longer than it should have.

Their mother steered down the middle, eyes moving constantly—waterline, rock, tree trunks, the place where floating debris could hide a log just under the surface. She didn't swerve for smaller things. She let the bow split them and kept the boat steady, like she'd decided wobbling was the real danger.

Brian stayed standing until his legs started to shake and then he sat hard on the bench, fingers locked around the rail.

The wake from another boat rolled through, low and heavy. It lifted them and dropped them again. Matt grabbed the seat edge and glanced back over his shoulder like he expected the cabin cruiser to be closer, like it might have followed them.

"People," Matt said, pointing.

Brian looked.

Two men stood on a dock farther down, shirts off, legs wide, one of them holding a flashlight even though the sun was still out. The beam skimmed the water in a slow sweep, not looking for fish. When it hit their boat, the man lifted his arm once—half wave, half question.

Their mother didn't wave back.

She didn't speed up either. She kept the same pace and passed without turning her head.

Brian watched the man's mouth open like he'd called something out. Wind carried nothing to them. The dock slid behind, then the next one, then the next.

A pontoon sat crooked on a lift, one corner down like a knee. A ski boat had been pulled too far up onto rock and now rested there awkwardly, its trailer tires half off the limestone. Someone had dragged a couch onto a porch and left it facing the channel as if watching the water might keep it from taking anything else.

The lake looked busy with aftermath in a way Brian had never seen.

He thought of their own dock, the rope, the cleat. He thought of his father's hands tying knots without looking. He wanted his father there, not to fix anything, but to make the day feel like it had edges.

Their mother kept her gaze forward.

The air smelled different after the storm—wet wood, torn leaves, gasoline from engines that had been run too hard and then shut off too fast. When she turned them into a narrow cut between two points, the water changed texture. It looked darker. Things gathered there—sticks, a child's plastic bucket, a clump of moss that might have been a towel.

Scott leaned forward and said, "Mom."

She glanced at him. "I see it," she said, and angled the boat a few degrees without losing speed.

Brian watched her hands on the wheel. Her knuckles were pale. Her forearms were tense. She looked like she was driving, not boating.

He remembered her teaching them to swim when they were smaller—one hand under your belly, the other steady on your back, voice calm no matter what was happening.

Matt opened his mouth like he wanted to tell her he'd been scared.

Instead he said, "Do you think Dad saw the tornado?"

Their mother didn't answer right away.

"He's fine," she said finally. Not because she knew. Because she needed it to be true.

The engine picked up. The lake widened again. The wreck receded until it looked less impossible, then smaller, then like just another shape on the shore.

Later, Brian knew, there would be voices on docks and porches that tried to make it smaller.

Lucky, someone would say, shaking their head like it was just weather. Boats like toys. Could've been worse.

Brian kept his eyes on the life jacket and the torn canvas and the pale scars on the cliff face. He held onto those instead. He didn't know what else was true.

They rode the rest of the way in silence, their own cove coming into view calm and ordinary, the wreck already behind them.

CH 14

High Water Line

WHEN THEY REACHED their dock, Rick was already there. He stood with one hand on the cleat, staring out at the channel like he could see through rain and distance. His shirt clung to his chest. Water ran off the brim of his hat in a steady line.

"You all right?" his father said.

No one answered right away. The question was too big for how it was asked.

His mother tied the boat off fast, the way she did everything when she didn't want space for anyone else's panic. The rope bit into her fingers and she didn't react. Brian stepped onto the dock carefully, bare feet finding the boards like they were a test. He kept his hands closed.

His father's eyes flicked down to those hands. "Let me see," he said.

"They're fine," Brian said, too quick.

His father didn't argue. He looked out at the lake again, jaw working once. "Damn weather," he muttered, like the sky could hear him.

Inside the cabin, everything smelled wet.

Not just wood and lake water. Wet cloth. Wet skin. Damp shoes. The screens rattled in the window frames when the wind moved through, even after the worst of it had passed.

His mother opened drawers like she was checking inventory. Towels came out. Dry shirts. A roll of paper towels. She moved around them, hands busy, face steady.

"Sit," she told Matt, not unkind.

Matt sat on the edge of the couch and stared at his own knees. His legs bounced. He didn't seem to know he was doing it.

His father walked through the room and stopped at the kitchen table. On it were the same things as always: a chipped ashtray, a stack of mail that didn't belong here, a fishing license folded twice. He picked up the license and shook it once, then set it down carefully.

He slid the mail into a tighter stack and set the fishing license under it so it wouldn't get damp. Small order, on purpose.

Scott stood in the doorway between rooms, watching.

His father opened the screen door and looked out at the porch roof. "We lost a shingle," he said.

No one replied.

"That's money," his father added, louder, like the problem had to be named before it could be fixed. "If it leaks, that's money."

His mother didn't say yes. She didn't say no. She tore a paper towel off the roll and handed it to Brian.

Brian took it without opening his hands.

"Go rinse," his mother said.

Brian went to the sink and held his fists under the tap, water running over knuckles and down the drain. He didn't look at anyone.

Scott watched his mother's face when she thought no one was looking. The way it tightened and then smoothed again. The way she breathed in through her nose, slow, and let it out like she was counting.

"Was it close?" he asked before he could stop himself.

His mother looked at him.

For a second he thought she might answer honestly. Not with a story. Just with a word.

Instead, she said, "Get your shoes off. You're tracking mud."

Brian turned off the faucet. He peeled the wet paper towel from his palms and threw it away quickly, like evidence.

His father walked past him and opened the cabinet under the sink, pulling out a flashlight and setting it on the counter. He grabbed a hammer from the drawer without looking.

"Power's still on," he said, and then, like it meant there was still a way to keep going.

His mother started making food without asking if anyone was hungry. Bread in the skillet. Butter. The smell rose warm and ordinary, cutting through wet wood.

For a minute, it worked.

Matt stopped bouncing his leg. Brian leaned his shoulder against the wall and closed his eyes. Scott watched his father's hands move over the counter, touching things, putting them down, touching them again, like he was learning the room by feel.

Outside, a branch scraped the cabin once and then stopped.

No one said tornado.

No one said scared.

They ate standing up, quiet, listening to the lake settle back into its usual sounds as if it had never changed at all.

* * *

After dark, the power stayed on, but the lights felt thin.

The porch bulb threw a small yellow circle onto wet boards. Beyond it, the yard was black and soft, the trees a wall. The lake was there only by sound—water against rock, a dock tapping somewhere down the cove, an engine starting far off and then stopping again.

Rick set the flashlight on the porch rail and tested it with a click. The beam cut white through the dark, sharp-edged.

"Hold this," he said to Scott, and didn't wait for an answer.

Scott took the flashlight and pointed it where his father nodded. The roofline. The corner where the shingle had lifted.

Rick climbed onto the porch rail the way he climbed onto anything—quick, decisive, as if hesitation was a kind of weakness. He swung one leg up and then the other, boots slipping once on the wet wood.

Scott's stomach dropped.

"Careful," he said.

Rick grunted, not agreement, just sound. He crawled onto the lower slope of the roof and stopped where the beam landed.

Up close, the roof looked like skin that had been scraped. Leaves stuck to shingles. A branch had dragged across it and left a clean line through grit.

Rick lifted the loose shingle and peered under it, flashlight glare cutting into his eyes. He held the hammer in his other hand like a promise.

"Nails pulled," he said. "Wind got under it."

Scott didn't say anything. He only kept the light steady and watched his father's hands.

Rick reached into his pocket and pulled out a few nails. He set them in a row on the shingle, then realized he couldn't reach them with the hammer without losing balance.

"Hand me one," he said.

Scott's hands were empty.

He looked down at the porch, then back up at the roof, and felt the uselessness of being asked to help without being given anything to give.

Rick said, sharper, "A nail."

Scott glanced toward the screen door. Through it he could see Linda moving in the kitchen, her outline crossing the window once, then stopping.

"Mom," Scott called, not loud.

The screen door opened and Linda stepped onto the porch, dish towel over her shoulder. She looked up at Rick on the roof without changing her face.

"What," she said.

Scott said, "Nails."

Linda stepped to the porch rail, reached up, and took two nails from Rick's hand where he'd already moved them to a better place without noticing he'd done it. She handed them to Scott. Her fingers brushed his.

Scott held one between thumb and forefinger and lifted it up.

Rick took it without looking, set it, and tapped it in with two quick hits. The hammer sounded hard and final in the dark. He drove the second nail in deeper, then flattened the shingle with his palm.

He sat back on his heels and looked out over the lake.

Scott followed his gaze.

Across the channel, a few lights had come on—porch bulbs, lanterns, one bright floodlight that made a dock look like a stage. Shadows moved under it. People were awake. People were counting what was missing.

Rick said, "I heard a boat hit rock down by the point."

Linda didn't answer.

Rick waited like he expected her to fill in the story for him. "Did you see anything out there?" he asked. His voice was controlled, but Scott heard the strain in it.

Linda said, "We came home."

Rick's jaw worked once. He nodded like that was enough.

Scott kept the light on his father's hands. On the dirt under his nails. On the wetness on his knuckles that wasn't from rain.

Rick wiped his forehead with the back of his wrist and then pointed with his chin toward the channel. "Millstone Lodge probably got tore up," he said, as if naming another place would keep theirs safe. "They got those big windows."

Scott pictured something he'd never seen—glass, lights, a lobby full of people who didn't live on the lake. He didn't know why his father thought of it now.

Linda said, "We're not there."

Rick nodded again. He shifted his weight forward and began crawling back toward the porch, movements careful now that the job was done.

Scott backed up a step to make room.

When Rick dropped back onto the porch rail, he did it with a small grunt like pain, or effort, or both. He stood and took the flashlight from Scott's hand.

He clicked it off.

Darkness came back fast, full.

Rick said, "Everybody's fine," not as a question.

Linda turned toward the screen door. "Shoes," she said to Scott, like that was the only thing she could correct. "Off."

Scott stepped inside and did what she told him.

Behind him, the porch boards creaked once under his father's weight, then went still.

CH 15

Hourglass

MATT WATCHED OWEN pick his way along the seawall stones and felt his throat tighten.

Owen moved like it was nothing—one foot, then the other, toes finding flat spots, hands out for balance without thinking about what his fingers might touch. The rocks looked the same as they always did. Warm. Ordinary. Full of cracks.

"Stay up," Matt said.

Owen glanced back, annoyed. "I am."

Matt didn't say why. He only kept his eyes on the gaps between slabs until the boy climbed back onto the level stones and pretended he'd never been close to slipping.

A day or two after the storm, the boys didn't talk about snakes until they had to.

Adults said things like watch where you step and be careful in the same flat tone they used for don't slam the screen door. The words were supposed to do the work by themselves.

It was late in the day and the heat had settled into the rocks. The seawall along the shoreline held it and gave it back. The limestone was warm under their palms when they sat and leaned over the edge.

Matt liked skipping rocks because it was simple. Find a flat one. Flick it. Count the hits. He could do it without thinking too hard, and thinking too hard was what got him in trouble.

Brian stood a few feet away with his hands on his hips, scanning the water the way their father did. Scott crouched and sorted rocks by feel, turning them over in his hands, rejecting most of them without throwing.

The lake was quieter than it had been the night of the storm. No wind. Just the small slap of water against stone and the distant whine of a boat engine somewhere out on the channel.

"Bet I can get eight," Matt said.

"No you can't," Brian said.

Matt threw anyway. The rock hit once, twice, three times, then sank with a small sound.

"Three," Scott said, not looking up.

Matt's face flushed. He walked along the rocks, hunting for a better one, shoes scuffing, toes searching for balance. The seawall stones were set like steps. He'd been on them a hundred times. He didn't think of them as dangerous.

He stepped down into a gap between two slabs and felt something sharp against his hand when he reached out to steady himself.

He jerked back fast.

"Ow," he said, more surprised than hurt.

Brian turned. "What'd you do?"

Matt held his hand out, palm up. Two small marks sat near the base of his thumb, clean as pinpricks. For a second it looked like nothing.

"I got scratched," he said.

Scott saw the marks and felt his stomach drop in a slow, heavy way.

"Don't move," Scott said.

Matt blinked at him. "It doesn't even hurt."

Scott didn't answer. He looked down into the rocks where Matt had stepped.

Half-coiled between the limestone slabs, a copperhead lay so still it could have been part of the pattern. Copper and leaf-brown, the hourglass shapes running down its back like somebody had painted them on for camouflage. Its head was angled toward the gap. It didn't rattle. It didn't warn. It simply owned the space it was in.

Brian moved too fast, grabbing Matt's wrist and yanking him back up onto the higher rock. Matt yelped, more at the grip than the bite.

"Hey—"

"Stop," Scott said, voice tight. "Don't squeeze it. Don't—"

Matt looked from one face to the other. Then the burn arrived.

His mouth opened without sound.

"It burns," he said finally, small.

Brian's grip loosened immediately, like he'd been holding a hot pan. He shifted his hands so he was supporting Matt's forearm without pressing.

"Mom," Scott said, and the word sounded wrong in his mouth.

Brian didn't argue. He scooped Matt up under the knees and back the way he carried him when he was pretending it was a joke. This wasn't a joke. Matt's body went stiff in his arms.

Scott kept his eyes on the rocks as they moved away, watching for the snake to move, for it to follow, for it to do anything. It stayed where it was, quiet, as if it had already forgotten them.

The path through the trees back to the cabin was narrower than it had been that morning. Branches slapped their arms. Leaves stuck to Matt's damp forehead.

Brian ran anyway.

He shouted before they reached the porch. "Mom!"

Their mother came out fast, dish towel in her hand. She took one look at Matt's face and then at his hand.

"Sit," she said. "Right here."

Brian set him down on the porch step like he was placing something breakable. Matt tried to pull his hand to his chest. His mother caught his wrist gently and held it steady.

She didn't do anything dramatic. No yelling. No stories. She rinsed the hand at the porch spigot, water running over the marks and down onto the dirt. She wrapped it with a clean cloth from the kitchen drawer, firm and higher than it needed to be.

"You're going to be okay," she said, already calling for the keys.

Their father wasn't there. He was off somewhere at the dock or in the shed. It didn't matter. Their mother was already calling for the keys.

"Get in the car," she told them.

* * *

The drive felt longer than the road was.

It was the station wagon, warm inside and smelling faintly of groceries and sunscreen.

Matt sat in the back seat with his bitten hand propped on a pillow. His other hand held his wrist like he could keep the pain from climbing. He stared at the cloth wrapping as if he could see through it.

Scott sat beside him, watching the swelling creep and then pause and then creep again, slow as a tide. He tried to memorize it. He didn't know why. It made him feel like there was something to do.

Brian sat up front and kept his jaw locked. He stared out the windshield and replayed the moment his hand had closed around Matt's wrist. He couldn't tell if he'd helped or made it worse. He couldn't ask anyone. There was no place to put that question.

Their mother drove with both hands on the wheel, shoulders set. The road out of Horseshoe Bend curved and rose. Trees flashed by in green walls. The sun stuttered through branches, bright and then dark, bright and then dark.

At the clinic, the air smelled like floor cleaner and old coffee. A nurse asked questions their mother answered in short clean sentences. Matt's eyes followed every adult hand that reached for him.

The doctor looked at the bite and said words that didn't land—mild, observe, swelling, pain management. He talked like he was discussing weather. He didn't look alarmed. That almost made Matt more scared.

When the doctor touched the swollen hand, Matt cried.

Not loud at first. Then all at once, full-body, embarrassed by it even as it happened.

Their mother stood close enough that her leg pressed against his. She didn't tell him to stop. She kept her hand on his shoulder, steady.

* * *

On the drive back, Matt went quiet. His face looked tired, as if the crying had emptied him. He leaned his head against the window and watched the world pass without seeing it.

Back at the cabin, they walked down to the seawall again before dark.

Not because anyone said to. Because they needed to look.

The rocks were the same as they always had been. Warm, flat, ordinary. The gaps between slabs held shadow. The lake slapped gently at the base of the wall.

Matt stood with his wrapped hand held close to his chest. Brian stood between him and the rocks without thinking about it. Scott crouched and stared at the place where it had happened until his eyes started to make patterns out of nothing.

No snake showed itself.

Their mother called from the porch, "Wash up," like it was any other night.

Brian turned first and walked back without speaking.

Matt followed, careful with his steps.

Scott stayed one more second, listening to the water against stone, and then he turned away too.

CH 16

Under the Boards

WHEN BRIAN was fourteen, under the dock the water was always colder.
That was why they liked it there. The shade, the way the world went quiet as soon as you slipped past the edge. Above, the lake was bright and loud and full of glare. Under, it turned green and close. Light broke into long ribbons that moved when the boards shifted.

They took turns diving through.

Matt went first, always. He was small enough to slip between the foam floats without scraping. He came up on the other side grinning, hair slicked flat, laughing like he'd proven something.

"Nothing there," he said. "It's fine."

Scott followed, slower, eyes open the whole way. He counted the foam blocks as they passed. White, scarred, chewed at the corners by years of bumping. He surfaced with less enthusiasm and wiped water off his eyes with the heel of his hand.

Brian waited last.

He sat on the dock edge with his legs in the water and listened. The boards were warm under his thighs. The lake tapped at the floats in a steady rhythm. Somewhere out on the channel a boat engine rose and fell, then disappeared.

"Your turn," Matt called.

Brian didn't answer. He pushed off and slid in clean.

The water closed over his head and the sound dropped away. For a moment it was only pressure in his ears and the familiar sight of foam sliding past above him. His hands moved out in front of him, slow, not touching, just feeling where the space was.

Then something moved where nothing had moved before.

Not fast. Not sudden. A shift in the dark between two blocks of styrene.

He stopped swimming.

Momentum carried him forward anyway, slow and wrong, the dock narrowing above him. He could feel the space tightening around his shoulders. His lungs burned with the urge to kick hard and be done with it.

In the gap, a thick body lay coiled, barely visible until it was. Dark and heavy. The head lifted slightly, mouth closed. The eyes didn't give him anything.

The snake didn't strike.

It didn't retreat.

It held its place.

Brian felt his throat tighten. He could hear his own heartbeat, loud in the water. He pushed gently backward, hands sweeping through the green like he was afraid to wake something. His heel brushed foam and he flinched so hard his stomach turned.

The snake flexed once, not toward, not away. Just enough.

He kicked again, careful, and slid back into the light.

He broke the surface too fast and gulped air that tasted thin and hot.

"What?" Matt said, already laughing, relief too quick. "What's wrong with you?"

Brian hauled himself onto the dock, palms slapping wet boards, chest heaving. He stared down into the gap where the water went dark again.

Scott leaned over beside him. "What did you see?"

Brian shook his head once. Then again. "We're done," he said.

Matt snorted. "You scared yourself."

They leaned over together, peering down.

For a long second there was nothing—just water, shadow, the white edge of foam. Matt's mouth started to form another laugh.

Then the head rose.

Just enough to be unmistakable. Flat and still.

No one moved.

Matt's laugh died in his throat.

The snake slipped back into the dark without sound.

Brian's hands stayed on the dock boards. He could feel the grain under his palms, rough and familiar, and suddenly that didn't mean safe.

"Side," he said, and his voice came out steady.

They climbed out of the water without talking. Towels were forgotten. Skin prickled with cold that had nothing to do with temperature.

*　*　*

Later, when they went down to swim again, Brian didn't say why.

He just made rules with his body.

He stepped in from the side of the dock where the water was open. He kept them wide of the floats. When Matt started to angle toward the shaded gap out of habit, Brian caught his shoulder and pushed him outward without looking at his face.

"Quit," Matt said, annoyed, trying to turn it into a joke.

Brian said, "No," and the word ended it.

Scott watched Brian's eyes now, the way they stayed on the gaps between boards, on the places where the water went dark, on the foam blocks that looked clean from above and chewed up close.

They didn't tell their parents.

It wasn't a decision they made out loud. It was just what happened.

That night, Brian lay in bed and listened to the dock tap beneath the window. He felt the pressure of the dock ceiling above his head again, low and close, and the quiet watching from the dark place under it.

He kept his hands open on the sheet.

He didn't sleep fast.

CH 17

Nails and Lumber

AFTER THE STORM, Scott used what it left behind.
The boards weren't new. Nothing was new. It was scrap plywood warped by water, two-by-fours split at the ends, nails pulled crooked and hammered back in because there weren't enough to waste. When you carried the wood through the woods it smelled like wet sap and sun and the faint sweet rot of things that had started to go soft.

Scott found the first good piece near the shoreline where debris had washed up and snagged on brush. It was a plank with paint on one side, white and blistered. He ran his fingers along the edge and felt the splinters lift.

"That'll work," Brian said, and took it from him like it was already his.

They chose a tree back from the cabin, thick-trunked and older than all of them. Low branches forked wide enough to stand on. The bark was rough and warm. You could climb it without thinking.

They didn't call it a tree house at first.

Brian called it a platform.

Matt called it a fort.

Scott didn't call it anything. He watched the tree and pictured weight.

Brian climbed first, always. He tested branches with his foot before he committed, shifting his weight slowly until he felt which ones held and which ones gave. He worked quiet and fast, hammer tucked into his waistband, nails in his mouth for a second at a time until Scott told him to stop doing that.

"You'll swallow one," Scott said.

Brian spat the nail into his palm and didn't answer.

Matt hauled boards from the pile and dragged them through leaves, making too much noise. He liked the sound of building. It made him feel included.

"Don't drop them," Brian said.

Matt dropped one anyway, not on purpose, just because it was heavy and he was small.

The board hit the ground with a crack that startled birds out of a nearby branch. Matt flinched and then looked around like he expected to get in trouble with an adult.

No adult came.

Scott held one end of a two-by-four while Brian nailed the other end into place. Each hit of the hammer traveled through the wood and into Scott's arms. He could feel when the nail bent by the change in resistance, the faint give that meant the metal had turned.

"That one's bad," he said.

Brian kept hammering until the nail finally went in at an angle. "It's fine," he said.

Scott didn't argue. He watched the slight twist in the board, the way it didn't sit flush.

They built in layers, calling them levels like that made it solid.

The first level was just two boards nailed across a forked branch. Something you could stand on, barely. It felt like a victory anyway.

Matt climbed up onto it and bounced once, grinning.

"Don't," Scott said.

Matt froze mid-bounce, offended. "I wasn't."

Brian didn't look down. "Stop messing around," he said, like he was talking about a job.

Matt climbed down, sulking.

When the platform was wide enough to sit on without your knees touching bark, Brian leaned out and looked through the trees toward the lake. He could see the water in bright pieces. The cabin roof looked smaller from here. The dock looked like a line drawn in pencil.

"You can see everything," Matt said, climbing back up and trying to sound like the view belonged to him too.

Scott watched Brian's face. Brian liked the height. He liked being above.

Scott didn't like how the branches moved when Brian shifted his weight.

He put his hand on the main board and felt the vibration of their bodies through it.

"We need another brace," he said.

Brian said, "Later."

Matt said, "It's fine," and kicked his heel against the wood like a test.

Scott grabbed his ankle without looking up. Not hard. Just enough to stop it.

Matt jerked his foot back and glared.

Scott let go and went quiet.

* * *

The three of them worked until the light started to go flat and the woods filled with insects.

On the ground, Scott lined nails up on a rock and straightened the bent ones with the back of the hammer. Each tap made a small sound. He kept his eyes on the metal and listened to the tree above him creak under his brothers' shifting weight.

Brian called down, "Board."

Scott lifted one end and passed it up. His arms shook with the effort. He watched Brian take it and set it in place with quick confidence.

"Hold it," Brian said.

Scott held it steady while the hammer fell.

The first nail went in clean.

The second one didn't.

It caught something soft in the wood and angled. The board pulled slightly away from where it wanted to sit. Scott felt it through his fingers, a tiny change that would matter later.

"That's crooked," he said.

Brian hit it again, harder, until it went. "It's in," he said.

Scott let go. He didn't say that it wasn't the same as right.

Matt climbed up again with a door they'd found, no handle, paint flaking. He held it like a shield.

"For the entrance," he said.

Brian laughed once, quick. Not kind, not mean. Just sound. "Fine," he said. "Put it over there."

Matt wedged the door against a branch and looked pleased, as if he'd added something important.

From the porch, their mother called their names for dinner.

Brian didn't answer right away. He looked at the platform, the uneven boards, the nails showing, the door leaning.

He wanted it finished. The unfinished parts bothered him.

"Tomorrow," he said, not to them, to the tree.

Scott climbed down last. His hands were sticky with sap. His fingers ached from holding boards steady.

Before he followed the others back toward the cabin, he looked up once more.

The platform sat in the branches like a promise.

When the wind moved through the leaves, it moved with it, just a little.

He watched until it settled again.

* * *

The next day, they went back up.

The platform had held through the night. That was all the proof Brian needed.

Scott carried a new piece of wood he'd found near the shed—straight, heavy, not warped. It had a faint smell of creosote and old sun.

"For a brace," Scott said, and held it up.

Brian glanced at it, then away. "Later," he said.

Matt climbed the trunk and sat on the first level, legs dangling, kicking the bark lightly. "It's fine," he said, repeating Brian's word like it was a shield.

Scott didn't answer. He set the board down and started sorting through nails again, straightening bent ones on a rock.

Brian climbed up with the hammer. He moved with more confidence today, like yesterday had made the tree belong to him.

"Board," he called.

Scott handed one up, arms straining. He watched Brian set it in place, watched the way Brian's foot pressed into the main plank, making it flex.

Scott felt the flex in his teeth.

"Hold it," Brian said.

Scott held the end steady and watched the nail go in.

The wood split slightly near the edge. A thin crack that ran half an inch and stopped.

Scott said, "Stop."

Brian paused, hammer lifted. "What."

Scott pointed. "It's splitting."

Brian leaned in, squinted, then shrugged. "It's fine," he said, and drove the nail anyway.

The crack lengthened. Not dramatic. Just enough to be real.

Matt said, "It's fine," again, too quick.

Scott looked at Matt. Matt avoided his eyes.

Scott climbed up onto the platform and crouched, testing the board with his hand. It held. It also moved, a small give that wouldn't matter until it did.

He said, "We need to brace it," quieter now.

Brian's face tightened. "We'll do it," he said, and Scott heard the lie in it. Not malicious. Just the kind of lie boys used when they didn't want to slow down.

Scott looked down.

From up here, he could see the cabin roof through leaves. He could see the dock and the cove. He could see their mother moving in the yard, small and steady, as if her body kept the place running by sheer repetition.

Scott held the platform's edge with both hands and listened.

The tree creaked softly under their shifting weight.

He couldn't tell if it was the tree talking or the boards.

He swallowed and said nothing.

He stayed close to the trunk, keeping his knees bent, keeping his body ready, as if readiness could make a structure safe.

When their mother called them in for dinner later, she didn't ask what they were building. She didn't look up at the branches.

Scott watched her move through the kitchen and waited for himself to say something anyway—to warn her, to make it real.

He didn't.

CH 18

The Long Drop

SCOTT HEARD the first creak from the yard and knew he was going to see something he didn't like.

Jake had dragged two boards under the big tree and set them across a low branch like it was a beginning. Emily stood a few feet back with her phone up, filming.

Scott said, "Hold it," and the words came out of his mouth before he decided to say them.

Scott knew it was wrong before it happened.

He felt it in the way the platform answered their weight—too much give, too much sound. Wood talked when it was under strain. You could hear the difference between a board settling and a board giving up.

They were back in the tree the next day, sweat already on their necks. The air was thick with insects. The storm had left the woods messy and generous. There was always one more board to drag in, one more nail to straighten on a rock, one more idea Matt had that sounded like a shortcut.

Brian climbed first and started hammering without asking if anyone was ready.

"Hold it," he called down.

Scott braced a board with both hands and felt the vibration of the hammer through the wood and into his wrists. Each strike was a small shock.

Matt climbed up onto the platform and stood where the boards overlapped. He wanted the height. He wanted to be seen up there.

"Don't move around," Scott said.

"I'm not," Matt said, and shifted his feet anyway, testing the give like he couldn't help it.

Scott looked at the nails along the edge. One was bent. Another sat too close to a split in the wood. He could see the grain opening around it, the crack already started, patient.

He opened his mouth to say brace it, or move it, or stop, and felt the words get lost behind the older brother's hammering.

Brian leaned down from above, eyes on the board. "It's fine," he said, like saying it made it true.

Scott tightened his grip and held the board as steady as he could.

Matt crouched, picked up the hammer, and started to tap a nail into the platform near his knee. His tongue stuck out in concentration. He liked being useful in the visible way.

Scott watched the branch under the platform. It flexed once, barely.

The crack came sharp and clean.

The sound ran straight through Scott's chest and into his teeth.

He saw it before the platform dropped: the split opening along the grain, the nail tearing sideways, the board lifting at the edge as if taking a breath.

"Wait—" he said.

The platform buckled.

It dropped once, then went.

Matt's eyes went wide. His mouth opened. One hand still held the hammer.

For a second he hung in the air with the board beneath him, suspended in a way that didn't belong to bodies.

Then gravity finished its work.

He fell with the plywood and the loose nails and the handle-less door they'd leaned against the trunk.

There was no scream. Just the rush of breath pulled out of him when he hit the ground hard enough that the woods went quiet.

Brian and Scott didn't move.

They watched him fall because they were still up in the branches and there was nothing to grab that would bring him back.

Scott's hands were still on the board he'd been bracing. Brian had one foot wedged on a branch and one hand gripping bark too hard.

Scott forced himself to move.

He climbed down too fast, branches scraping his arms, his shoe slipping on bark. Brian dropped beside him, landing heavy, not caring where his feet went.

Matt lay on the ground with plywood scattered around him like it had never belonged together. The hammer was in the leaves a few feet away.

His eyes were open.

His chest moved once, then again, shallow.

Brian knelt beside him and stopped his hands in the air, not knowing where to put them. "Don't move," he said, voice tight.

Matt's mouth worked. "I dropped—" he said, and coughed. "I dropped the hammer."

Scott looked at the angle of his arm and felt his stomach turn cold.

"Can you feel your feet?" he asked.

Matt nodded. Then shook his head. Then nodded again, confused by his own body.

"It hurts," he said finally, small.

"I know," Scott said.

He didn't touch him. He only hovered his hands near the places that looked wrong, trying to hold the shape of Matt in place with air.

Brian looked up at the tree, at the broken platform above them, and then back down, jaw clenched so hard his cheeks jumped.

"Mom," Brian said, and his voice cracked on the word.

He took off running toward the cabin.

Scott stayed on the ground beside Matt and listened to his breathing, counting it without meaning to.

Leaves stuck to Matt's sweaty forehead. His eyes stared past Scott into the branches overhead, as if he was still up there.

"Don't go to sleep," Scott said, not knowing if that was a real rule or just a thing people said.

Matt blinked slowly. "I'm not," he whispered.

* * *

Linda arrived first.

She ran through the trees with her hands up, not to touch anything, not yet. She looked once at the broken boards on the ground and then at Matt's face.

"What happened?" she asked, already kneeling.

Brian stood behind her, breathing hard, eyes too bright, jaw working.

"He fell," Scott said.

Linda looked at Matt's arm and didn't flinch. She touched his wrist gently, two fingers, checking without making it a big thing.

"Can you move your fingers?" she asked.

Matt tried. His face tightened and a sound came out of him that wasn't crying yet.

"Okay," Linda said. "Okay."

She looked up at Brian. "Go get towels. And the keys."

Brian didn't move at first. His eyes were still on Matt, like he couldn't let go of the sight or it would change.

"Now," their mother said, and Brian moved.

She looked at Scott next. "Stay with him," she said. "Don't let him try to sit up."

Scott nodded.

The mother slid her hand under Matt's shoulder and adjusted him an inch, just enough to make him more comfortable, careful as if he were glass.

"Breathe," she told him. "Just breathe."

Matt stared at her and tried to do what she said. His breath came in short pulls anyway.

The father arrived later, coming fast from the direction of the dock, shirt half-buttoned, hat in his hand.

He took in the scene in one look—the boards, the nails, Matt on the ground, their mother's hands steady on his shoulder—and his face hardened.

"Jesus Christ," he said, not at Matt, not at Brian. At the tree.

He pointed toward the broken platform above them. "I told you not to build up there," he said.

No one answered.

Their mother didn't look up. She said, "Get the car."

The father stood still a beat, as if deciding whether to argue, then turned and walked away through the leaves without another word.

Brian came back with towels and dropped them beside his mother's knee. His hands shook when he tried to unfold one.

Scott looked at Matt's eyes again. They were still open. Still here.

Matt whispered, "Is it broke?"

No one said yes.

No one said no.

Their mother smoothed his hair back once with the flat of her hand, quick and practical, and then went still again, waiting for the car to return.

Above them, the broken boards in the tree creaked once in the wind and then went quiet.

* * *

Two days later, their mother said they were going for a drive.

She didn't call it getting out of the cabin. She didn't say it would do them good. She packed sandwiches in wax paper and told them to put on shoes that weren't flip-flops.

Matt's arm was wrapped and held close against his chest. The cloth itched under his shirt sleeve. Every time the car hit a bump, he tightened his jaw and pretended he didn't feel it.

The road in climbed and twisted. Trees flickered past in a blur of green. Scott watched the ditches and the places the ground fell away. He watched without naming it.

They parked in a lot that smelled like hot asphalt and sun-warmed needles. Beyond it, stone rose out of the trees—walls with empty windows, corners still square in places and broken in others, vines threading the gaps.

Rick said, "That's it," like it was a place you were supposed to know.

The steps were cool where shade held. Moss clung in the cracks, dark and damp.

"Stay together," their mother said.

Inside, sound changed. Their shoes on stone echoed once and then thinned. A bird moved somewhere above them.

Scott saw the stairwell that went down before Matt did. The opening looked darker than it should have been, the air coming up cool as breath.

Matt moved toward it anyway.

Brian caught his shirt with a quick hard grip. "No."

Matt turned his head, chin lifted. "Why?"

Brian didn't have anything clean to give him. He only held on.

Matt slipped free and put one shoe on the first step.

The sole hit moss and slid.

For a second the world tilted. Stone rushed close. Matt's good hand shot out and scraped along rough rock, fingers skidding.

Brian yanked him back hard enough that Matt stumbled onto the flat stone at the top, chest burning, palm stinging.

Scott stepped in and put a hand on Matt's shoulder to steady him. Matt's face was bright with anger and something else underneath it.

Their mother's voice cut through the space. "Matthew."

Matt flinched at his full name.

Rick stepped closer and looked at the stairwell and then at Matt's scraped hand. "Those are slick," he said, as if he were explaining a tool, not fear.

Their mother pulled a handkerchief from her purse and dabbed at the torn skin. Her fingers were quick and practical.

"You don't go down there," she said. Then she gave him the reason because she'd just watched how fast it could happen. "You slip, you crack your head, and nobody sees it fast enough."

Scott heard the words and felt them lodge somewhere behind his ribs.

Matt swallowed and nodded once, the way he nodded when there wasn't anything else that worked.

Outside again, the sunlight hit hard. The ruins stood behind them, silent and unmoved, as if none of it had happened.

CH 19

Ice Machine

MATT'S ARM STILL HURT when he pretended it didn't. The bruise had yellowed, but the pain came back in sharp flashes when he moved wrong. He kept his hand out of the way. He didn't want anyone saying careful.

On the way back from the day trip, Linda stopped at Tan-Tar-A for something she said they needed—an envelope at the office, a call she couldn't make from the cabin, a reason that sounded practical enough to end questions.

They could hear the arcade before they could see it.

Not lake-noise. Not the slow slap of dock water or the one engine moving steady down the channel. This was inside-noise—bells, a bright electronic song that repeated until it became part of your heartbeat, and the hard clatter of ice dropping somewhere behind a closed door.

Linda kept the three of them close through the lobby like it was a grocery store, one hand on the strap of her purse, the other flat between Matt's shoulder blades. The air smelled like carpet shampoo and sunblock. Men walked past in wet trunks and T-shirts that stuck to their chests. Kids ran barefoot, leaving little damp prints that dried almost as soon as they landed.

Rick stopped once under a ceiling fan and looked up as if the blades might tell him the time. "We'll find the office," he said, but he didn't sound sure.

Brian nodded like he understood the plan.

Scott watched the hallways—how they branched, how the sound changed at each turn. The resort felt like a maze built for people with money to waste and kids with energy to burn.

Matt felt the arcade before he found it. The noise pulled him the way fireworks did—like something in him wanted to be told what to do.

His arm itched under the wrap. He held it close to his ribs like he could keep it from being noticed.

"Stay where I can see you," Rick said, and he pointed with two fingers, not his whole hand, as if making it smaller would make it easier.

Linda pressed a folded paper into Rick's palm—something with a room number or an office number on it—and angled herself toward a desk where a woman in a blue blouse was already saying hello to someone else.

Rick hesitated. His eyes flicked from the desk to the hallway to his sons.

Brian took that hesitation and made it permission. "We'll be right there," he said, already moving.

Scott followed because Scott always did, and Matt followed because Matt never wanted to be the one left behind.

The arcade door was propped open with a rubber wedge. Inside, the light dropped and the air cooled. The smell changed—ozone and soda syrup and warm machine guts. The carpet was patterned in dark colors to hide spilled drinks and cigarette burns.

Brian fished in his pocket for coins. He had a few quarters, flat and warm. He didn't show where they'd come from, but Matt could tell they were not new.

"One each," Brian said, as if he were dividing rations.

Matt took his quarter and fed it into a pinball machine. The machine woke up with a flash and a ding and then immediately punished him with a ball that shot sideways and drained before he could learn the buttons.

"You're doing it wrong," Brian said.

Matt tried again anyway. The flippers kicked under his fingers like small animals.

Scott watched Brian slap the coin return once, out of habit, the way older kids did. It clacked without giving anything back. A strip of paper was taped to the side of one cabinet with initials and numbers written in pencil, smudged where fingers had dragged across it.

Scott stood back by the doorway, pretending he didn't care, but watching through the glass for their parents. Every time someone walked past in the hallway, the arcade noise thinned for a second and then filled back in.

That was when Matt saw them.

A boy leaned against a machine like it was holding him up. He had sun on his shoulders that didn't look accidental. His hair was lighter at the ends from chlorine or wind. A cigarette sat tucked behind his ear, unlit, like a prop he didn't need to use to prove the point.

A girl stood with one knee bent, foot braced against the wall. She held a paper cup of soda and stirred it with a straw, slow, eyes moving across the room like she already knew what everyone was about to do.

Matt recognized them—the same posture, the same way their attention made a room feel smaller.

The boy looked over at Brian and smiled like he was remembering a joke. "Horseshoe Bend," he said, not asking.

Brian's jaw tightened. "Yeah," he said, too casual.

The girl's gaze went to Matt's hands on the pinball buttons. "You boys always come over here?" she asked.

"Sometimes," Brian said.

That was a lie, but it was a useful one. The lie warmed him.

The boy nodded toward the hallway. "Ice machine's down past the pool," he said. "Spits cubes like hail when you hit it right."

Matt didn't know what that meant, but the way the boy said it made it sound like a secret you could own.

Scott's voice came low, aimed at Brian. "Mom said stay where she can see us."

Brian didn't look at him. "She can see us," he said, and he tilted his head toward the open door like the hallway counted as sight.

The girl laughed once, soft. "Your mom doesn't see past her errands," she said, not cruel, just stating something like weather.

Matt felt the words land. He looked toward the door and realized it was true—Linda's steps would carry her from desk to office to car without her eyes ever searching the corners.

The boy pushed off the machine. "Come on," he said, and started for the doorway like it was already decided.

Brian followed, because Brian never wanted to be the one who refused first.

Scott stayed half a second longer, and Matt saw him make a choice with his face—the kind of choice you made when you knew it was wrong but you also knew you'd be punished for being left behind.

They stepped into the hallway and the arcade noise fell away behind them.

The ice machine sat in an alcove beside a trash can. A plastic scoop hung from a chain.

The boy slapped the side of it, once, with his palm.

For a second nothing happened.

Then the machine groaned and the first cubes came out, clattering into the bin with a sound like gravel.

Matt's eyes widened. It did look like hail.

The girl took the scoop and filled her cup halfway, then tipped most of the ice back into the bin like it was a trick she didn't need anymore.

"Hit it again," the boy said to Matt.

Matt looked at Brian. Brian's face said don't make us look stupid.

Matt hit the machine with his good hand. Not hard enough.

"Harder," the boy said.

Matt hit it again, harder this time, and the cubes spilled out faster, loud and bright.

For a second it felt like power—the idea that you could strike something and make it give.

Then a voice behind them said, "Hey."

They turned.

A man stood at the end of the hallway in a polo shirt with a name tag pinned to the chest. He looked at them the way Rick looked at the speedboat rules—like he was already counting what could go wrong.

The boy's smile didn't change. "Machine was stuck," he said.

"That machine isn't for playing," the man said.

The girl put her cup down on the trash can. "We're going, Sherwin," she said.

Brian stepped forward. "We're with our parents," he said, too quick.

The man's gaze slid past them toward the lobby. "Then get back to them," he said.

They walked fast without running. The hallway seemed longer on the way back, and Matt kept expecting Rick's voice—his real voice, the one that carried across water and stopped them mid-movement.

But when they reached the lobby again, Linda was still at the desk, head bent, listening hard, signing something with a pen that didn't belong to her. Rick stood beside her, looking at a brochure like he was trying to make sense of it.

He glanced up when the boys returned. His eyes went to their faces first, not their hands.

"Where were you?" he asked.

Brian answered like a grown man. "Just in the arcade."

Linda didn't look up. "Fine," she said, and the word landed like a dismissal and a relief at the same time.

Matt felt his stomach drop, not because he'd been caught, but because he hadn't.

* * *

Back at the cabin, the dock looked calm and ordinary. The foam floats knocked once under the boards, then settled. Brian checked the boat rope like their father did, tugging it twice. Scott sat on the edge with his feet in the water, watching.

Matt hovered behind them with his good hand shoved in his pocket, his wrapped arm hot and itchy inside his sleeve.

"Where's Carl?" Brian asked, not turning his head.

Matt didn't answer because he didn't know. Uncle Carl was supposed to be there by now. Brian kept looking out toward the channel like he could pull a boat into view just by watching hard enough.

Then a boat cut around the point and came into view, running too fast for the cove.

It was a ski boat, louder than their father's. The engine whined high. Two teenage boys stood on the back like they belonged there. A girl sat on the bow with her knees pulled up, hair lifting in the wind.

The boat slowed hard near the cove mouth, throwing a wake that rolled toward the dock.

The girl looked at them and smiled like she was already laughing at something.

The driver swung the boat in and cut the engine. Momentum carried it closer. The hull nudged the water, then rocked, then steadied.

"Hey," the driver called.

He was older than Brian by enough that it mattered. Sunburned shoulders. Cheap sunglasses. A cigarette tucked behind his ear the way the store clerk did.

Matt knew his name from the resort arcade.

Sherwin.

Sherwin pointed at the dock with his chin. "You boys coming?"

Brian didn't answer right away. He looked toward the cabin as if checking whether their father could see.

No one was on the porch.

Scott didn't move. He watched Sherwin's boat like he was measuring distance.

Heat claimed Matt's neck. Sherwin didn't come for little kids. If he was asking, it meant something.

"Where to?" Brian asked.

Sherwin grinned. "Cliffs."

The word landed like a dare all by itself.

Matt's mouth went dry.

Scott said, quiet, "We're not supposed to."

Sherwin didn't look at him. "Who says?" he asked.

Scott didn't answer.

Sherwin's eyes flicked to Matt's arm. "What'd you do?" he asked.

Matt lifted his chin. "Nothing," he said.

The girl on the bow laughed. Not loud. Just enough.

Sherwin nodded like that was the right answer. "Hop in," he said.

Brian hesitated one more second, then stepped onto the boat.

Matt followed immediately so no one could see him hesitate.

Scott came last, eyes on the dock as if memorizing how to get back.

* * *

The cliffs rose out of the lake like a wall.

Not straight, but tall enough that looking up made the back of Matt's neck tighten. The rock was pale limestone streaked with darker lines where water had run. People stood on ledges and moved like it was nothing, bare feet on stone, bodies outlined against the sky.

Sherwin killed the engine and let them drift near the base where the water went dark.

Matt looked down and couldn't see the bottom.

Other boats were already there, tied off or circling slow, music playing from speakers. Laughter carried off the rock and came back distorted. Every so often someone jumped and the water swallowed them with a slap that echoed.

Matt's chest buzzed like a swarm of bees.

The girl on the bow—Angie, he realized, because Sherwin said it once without looking at her—kicked her feet against the fiberglass and watched the jumpers like she'd seen it all and still wanted to see it again.

"You ever jumped?" she asked, eyes on Matt like she already knew the answer.

Matt swallowed. "Yeah," he lied.

Angie smiled wider. "From where?"

Matt pointed at a ledge halfway up. Not the highest. Not the lowest. Somewhere that sounded believable.

Sherwin laughed. "Sure you have," he said.

Brian stood near the windshield with his hands gripping the frame. He wasn't smiling. His eyes tracked each jump like he was counting outcomes.

Scott sat low, arms around his knees, staring at the rock face.

Sherwin leaned back and said to no one in particular, "You boys wanna be men, you gotta get wet."

The words weren't a joke. They were a rule.

Matt felt his arm itch inside the bandage. He could feel the bruise under it, still tender. He pictured the fall again—the crack, the air, the ground coming up.

He pushed it away.

Sherwin pointed at a lower ledge closer to the water. "That one's for kids," he said, and grinned at Angie. "You can go from there."

Matt's face burned.

He looked at Brian, waiting for Brian to say no.

Brian didn't look at him.

He looked at the ledge.

Scott looked at Matt's arm and then looked away.

Matt watched Brian look past him, watched Scott look away.

He pulled his shirt sleeve higher over the bandage like he was hiding it from the sun.

"Fine," he said.

Sherwin swung the boat closer and told him where to put his hands on the rock.

The limestone was warm and rough against Matt's palm. It scraped a little. He climbed up awkwardly, favoring his sore arm without admitting it, feet finding small ledges, toes gripping.

On the lower shelf, he stood and looked down at the water.

It didn't look that far.

Then he looked again and it did.

"Jump," someone called.

He couldn't tell who.

He heard Angie laugh once, sharp.

Matt's stomach rolled.

He held his arms out for balance and felt the bandage pull tight.

He thought about backing down and felt the shame hit first, hot and fast.

So he stepped off.

For a second there was no sound at all.

Then the lake hit him hard enough to punch the air out of his chest.

Cold water filled his ears. His eyes opened and saw green and bubbles and nothing else. His body flailed once out of instinct and his sore arm screamed.

He kicked hard and broke the surface, gasping, coughing, hair plastered to his face.

Sherwin whooped.

Angie clapped once, slow.

Brian smiled quickly, a flash of relief he couldn't hold.

Scott didn't smile. He watched Matt swim back toward the boat like he was checking that all his pieces still worked.

When Matt hauled himself over the side, water streaming off him, his chest still hurt from the impact.

Sherwin slapped him on the shoulder, not gentle. "There you go," he said.

Matt laughed with them because that was the rule too.

* * *

On the ride back, Matt sat on the floor of the boat with his back against the seat base, shivering in the wind.

His sore arm throbbed inside the bandage. He held it close to his ribs so it wouldn't move.

Brian stood near the console again, watching the water ahead. Scott sat beside Matt and didn't speak.

Sherwin drove fast.

The cliffs got smaller behind them. The rock face turned into a pale line, then into nothing.

Matt kept looking back anyway.

He wanted to remember the moment he stepped off the ledge the way it felt in the air—before the water hit, before the coughing, before the pain.

That part felt clean.

When they slipped back into the cove, the cabin was visible through the trees. Smoke rose thin from a grill somewhere down the shore. The dock waited.

Sherwin cut the engine and let the boat glide in.

"Don't tell your old man," Sherwin said, like it was casual.

Brian nodded once.

Matt nodded too fast.

Scott didn't nod at all.

As Matt stepped onto the dock, his legs went a little weak. He gripped the rail with his good hand until the world steadied.

He didn't say anything about it.

He followed his brothers up the steps toward the cabin, water dripping off him onto the boards, and kept his eyes on the porch so he wouldn't turn around and look at the cliffs again.

CH 20

The Ledge

A COUPLE DAYS LATER, the cliffs were loud before you could see them.

Music flattened against rock and came back thin. Engines ran in uneven bursts—rev, cut, rev. Nobody could decide whether to stay or leave. Wakes crossed and crossed again until the surface stopped looking like water and started looking like broken glass.

By then, the summer had gone long enough that rules started to feel optional if nobody was watching.

When they finally slid close enough, the limestone looked bleached in the sun, streaked darker in places where water had run down and dried.

Brian kept them out of the worst of it as best he could.

He stood at the bow with one hand on the rail and watched boats slide too close, watched prop wash boil white behind sterns, watched the way people didn't look where they were going because they expected the water to carry them anyway.

Scott sat low by the console, eyes moving constantly, mapping paths through the traffic. Matt leaned over the side and dragged his fingertips through the water until Brian slapped his hand away without turning his head.

"Quit," Brian said.

Matt rolled his eyes, but he stopped.

They were younger than they should have been to be out here alone, and they knew it. Their father had said the words fast and final—stay out of the channel, don't get close to the cliffs, if there's trouble you come straight back. The rules had been delivered the way tools were handed over. Here. Use it right.

They weren't supposed to be this close.

But boats kept drifting toward the rock face, and the sound of it pulled them with the rest. If you stayed back, you couldn't see. If you couldn't see, you didn't count.

Sherwin's ski boat was there, idling a little off to the side, too glossy and loud for the hour. Angie sat on the bow with her feet on the fiberglass, hair lifting in the wind. She didn't look at them. She didn't have to.

Brian tried not to look at the ledges above.

People stood up there in swimsuits and bare feet, bodies outlined against the bright sky. Every so often someone ran and launched out, and the crowd on the boats shouted and laughed and made the jump into a story before the jumper even hit the water.

Brian watched the distance anyway. He measured without meaning to.

Scott leaned forward. "We should go," he said.

Brian didn't answer, because leaving felt like losing.

That was when the shout cut through everything else.

Not one of theirs.

A man stood on the deck of a cabin cruiser near the rock face, arms waving hard, pointing down. His voice cracked with effort. You couldn't make out the words at first, only the shape of panic.

Then a woman screamed a name.

Boats shifted. Engines surged and cut. Someone threw a rope that slapped the water and sank short. Another voice shouted instructions that contradicted the first.

"What's happening?" Matt asked.

Brian's throat tightened. He scanned the surface near the rock, eyes trying to catch movement in chop and glare.

The lake looked the same as it had a minute ago. Busy. Bright. Nothing marked.

"There," Scott said, and his voice shook. "By the rock."

Brian saw it then—not a full body, not a clear shape. A head breaking the surface and slipping under again too fast to follow. Dark hair. An arm. Or maybe the wave had made it look like an arm.

Brian's chest went cold.

Not a little kid. A teenage boy, shoulders narrow, hair plastered to his face.

Nobody sees it fast enough, a part of him said, and he didn't know where the words had come from until he felt his palms start to sweat.

He leaned forward, already doing the math, already feeling his legs prepare. He could jump. He could reach. He could—

"Don't," Scott said.

Brian turned his head just enough to see Scott's face. Scott wasn't looking at him. He was looking at the water like he was trying to hold it with his eyes.

Matt stood up, eyes wide. "We have to help."

Brian looked for an adult who would tell them what to do.

No one did.

No one with a name tag. No one with keys.

Boats clustered tighter now, engines idling, wakes stacking into confused chop that lifted their bow and dropped it again. People shouted over each other. A man on another boat yelled, "Back up!" and then, "Get closer!" as if both could be true at once.

Brian felt the old urge rise—move, decide, make it not be this.

He grabbed the bow rail with both hands and leaned out to judge the drop. The water below was darker, the rock face throwing a shadow. He could see the distance from their boat to the spot where the head had been.

Not far.

Far enough.

The head surfaced again, farther out this time, and Brian saw a face for half a second—mouth open, eyes wide—and then it slipped under like it had been pulled straight down by its own weight.

Brian's hands went numb.

He started to climb the rail.

Scott grabbed the back of his shirt and yanked him down hard.

"No," Scott said into his shoulder. Not loud. Not begging. Just no.

Brian twisted, furious, and then stopped because Scott's grip didn't let go. Scott held him like he was holding a door shut.

"Let go," Brian said.

Scott didn't answer.

On the cabin cruiser, the woman screamed the name again. It sounded smaller the second time.

Someone jumped in.

There was a splash and then another head and another set of arms thrashing in the chop, and someone shouted for them to get out.

Brian's stomach rolled.

A siren sounded somewhere distant, thin and late.

The boats began to back off in an uneven ripple, not all at once. Engines revved. Hulls turned. The water changed shape as the wakes unstacked and then stacked again in new places.

Brian felt their boat drift with the current, pulled away without choice. He could still see the rock face. He could still see the place where the head had been, even though there was no mark now, only water and glare.

Scott kept one hand on Brian's shirt for a long moment even after Brian stopped trying to climb.

Matt started to cry without making any noise. Tears ran down his cheeks and mixed with spray.

Brian didn't look at either of them.

He stared at the water until his eyes hurt.

* * *

The ride back to Horseshoe Bend was quieter than it should have been for a holiday.

Their engine sounded small in the open channel. Brian kept it steady and didn't look toward other boats. Scott sat low and held onto the seat edge with both hands. Matt wrapped his arms around himself and watched the shoreline pass without blinking.

When the dock finally came into view, Brian eased in too fast, then corrected, embarrassed by it. The boat bumped once against a post.

No one said anything.

On the dock, Brian's legs didn't feel like his.

He untied the rope and tied it again, knot too tight, hands working hard like the rope was the problem. Scott stood beside him and watched without offering help.

Matt climbed the steps toward the cabin with wet footprints on the boards and didn't look back.

Brian finished the knot and pulled on it once.

It held.

* * *

Inside, the cabin smelled like fried food and sunscreen, like other people's holidays.

Voices came from down the shore. Laughter. Someone shouting across water as if nothing had happened.

Rick was at the kitchen table with a beer and a plate of something he'd already started eating. He looked up when the boys came in dripping.

"Where you been?" he asked, like it was a normal question.

Brian didn't hesitate. "Swimming," he said.

Rick nodded as if that settled it. "Dry off," he said. "Your mom's going to have you tracking water."

Linda's voice carried from the back room—something about towels, something about shoes—ordinary words doing ordinary work.

Matt stood by the sink and watched the water run off his arms and onto the floor. He didn't wipe it up. He didn't move.

Scott went to the bathroom and held his hands under the tap until the skin went pink. He watched the drain like it could take the image with it if he stayed long enough.

In the bedroom, the three of them lay on top of the sheets in damp shorts, too hot to pull the covers up, too tired to talk the way kids talked at night.

Matt said, finally, into the dark, "You were going to."

Brian didn't answer.

Matt's voice tightened. "You were going to jump."

Scott stared at the ceiling and felt the moment replay in his body—his fist in Brian's shirt, the shove, the weight of him coming down hard.

Brian said, flat, "I would've got him."

No one said the other thing: maybe not.

Matt turned on his pillow. "You wouldn't have let him," he said to Scott, and it wasn't a question.

Scott didn't answer. He listened to the dock tap under the window and pretended it was only the dock.

Later, when Matt's breathing finally slowed and Brian's went steady, Scott heard a floorboard creak in the hall.

He waited, then heard the screen door slap soft, then quiet again.

He pulled again anyway.

PART THREE

CH 21

The First Morning

THE MORNING AFTER Matt arrived, Scott had slept in short pieces.
Smoke from last night's coals still lived in his hair and on his shirt. Each time he closed his eyes, he saw water flashing with other people's lights, too close together to trust.

When he finally woke for good, it wasn't because he meant to.

The cabin did it. The same way it always had—light coming early through thin curtains, a board popping somewhere in the wall, the smell of damp wood that never fully dried.

He lay still for a moment and listened.

Across the water, someone's wind chime rang once and stopped, thin and metallic. It made him think of Our Lady of the Lake up by town, still keeping time for whoever showed up.

In the kitchen, a drawer slid open, then shut. A mug clinked against the counter. Water ran at the sink and stopped.

He got up and stepped into the hall. The floor was colder than he expected—the addition his parents had built after the boys left still didn't hold heat the way the old part did. In the living room, the ceiling fan turned slow and made its tired click once each rotation.

His father stood at the counter in sweatpants and a clean shirt, holding a paper coffee filter in both hands like it was a note he'd been given and couldn't read.

His mother was at the stove with a skillet heating, dish towel on her shoulder, hair pulled back.

His father looked up as if he'd been caught. "Morning," he said.

"Morning," Scott said.

His father nodded and looked back down at the filter. "Where do these go again?"

His mother didn't turn around. "In the basket," she said, calm.

His father stared at the coffee maker as if it had moved overnight. He lifted the lid. He set the filter in, then adjusted it three times, making sure the edge sat flat.

Scott watched his hands.

His father reached for the coffee can, paused, and looked around the counter like he'd lost it.

It was right in front of him.

His mother set the skillet down on another burner and slid the coffee can closer without saying anything. Not a rescue. Just moving the object into the path.

His father took it and didn't acknowledge the motion.

"Your brother's already outside," his mother said, as if this was the part of the morning that mattered. "He's looking at that line back there."

Scott nodded. He could already smell it—faint and sour through the screen door, something that didn't belong with breakfast.

"Kids up?" he asked.

His mother made a small sound that could have been a laugh. "They've been up," she said.

From outside came the high whine of a wave runner crossing the channel, then the drop of its engine note as it turned.

His father flinched slightly at the sound, then smoothed his face.

Scott said, "I'm going to the dock."

His father looked at him, searching. "Dock," he repeated, as if confirming a word.

"Just going to check," Scott said, and let it go.

* * *

The steps down to the dock felt steeper than they used to. Or his legs were different. He couldn't tell which.

The waterline was lower, pulled back from the shore. Rocks that used to stay under the surface sat exposed and dry, pale in the morning. Old timbers stuck up near the edge at angles, black with algae where the water had been and clean above, the split between the two like a tide mark on wood.

On the dock, Jake stood with his phone out, filming the wave runner as it looped back toward the channel. Emily sat cross-legged near the cleat, knees hugged to her chest, phone in her hand, thumb moving.

Emily looked up when she heard him. "Hi," she said, then looked back down.

At the top of the steps, Julie sat on the bench with a magazine she wasn't reading, watching the kids without calling down.

Jake didn't turn around. "Can I ride one of those?" he asked.

"No," Scott said.

Jake finally looked at him. "Why?"

Scott stared out at the water, at the wave runner's path, at how quickly it could take a kid out of sight.

He said, "Because they can take you out around the point before anybody even knows you turned. And people run the channel too fast."

Jake looked back at the water like the answer didn't fit the question.

Out past the cove mouth, a cigarette boat came around the point low and fast, chrome catching the sun, wake spreading in a V that would reach both shores. The engine noise arrived a half-beat behind the image, deep enough to feel in the dock boards.

Scott watched it until it passed. The wake hit the dock ten seconds later, lifting the boards, slapping the floats, then settling like nothing had happened.

Jake rolled his eyes like the answer was old-fashioned.

The wave runner swung wide and came back again, close enough that Scott could see the rider standing up.

Tyler from two cabins down. No life jacket. No hesitation. Just his knees bent and his head turned like the lake belonged to him.

The dock shifted under Scott's feet when a wake reached the cove mouth. The boards tapped against the floats. The sound traveled up through his shoes into his shins.

He leaned over and looked down at the floats under the dock—black plastic now, sealed and smooth where the white foam used to show its wear. The gaps between them looked tighter than they should have.

Jake stepped close to look too.

"Don't go under there," Scott said, quick.

Jake blinked at him. "I wasn't."

Scott put his hand flat on the dock board, grounding himself in the grain, and stood back up.

Behind him, the screen door slapped.

His father came down the steps slower than he used to, one hand on the railing, cup in the other. He stopped halfway down and looked at the dock as if measuring it.

"It's lower," his father said.

"Yeah," Scott said.

His father stepped onto the dock and walked toward the cleat where the rope was tied, the same rope, the same knot. He looked at it a long moment.

The boat was different, though. A Rinker deck boat with a bimini top and seating for eight, wide and stable where the old Glastron had been narrow and quick. Scott remembered how that Glastron used to lift in a wake, how you could feel the water thinking about coming over the side. This one just sat there.

"Did you—" he started, then stopped.

Scott waited.

His father cleared his throat. "Did you check that?" he asked, and the question sounded like it had been lifted from another year.

"It's fine," Scott said.

His father nodded too hard, as if that settled something.

The wave runner cut back across the channel and the engine note rose. Jake lifted his phone again, arm steady.

His father watched the wave runner for a beat, eyes narrowed, then looked away first.

He took a sip of coffee and made a face. "Cold," he said, and then smiled like it was a joke.

No one laughed.

* * *

In the yard behind the cabin, Brian had already turned the work into a job.

Tools lay arranged on an old towel—wrench, shovel, a pair of gloves, tape measure. The ground near the septic line was disturbed in a neat rectangle where he'd already started digging. The smell was stronger back here, not overwhelming, just present enough to make you keep your mouth shut.

Brian wiped sweat off his forehead with the back of his wrist. He nodded at Scott without looking up from the hole.

"We'll have to open it," Brian said.

Scott nodded. "When's the inspector?"

"Tuesday," Brian said. "Your mom says Tuesday. So we do what we can today. Tomorrow we see what we can't do and call someone who can."

It was a list. It was always a list with him.

Matt came out through the screen door with coffee in his hand and stopped at the edge of the yard. He'd rolled in the afternoon before—late, like he was doing everyone a favor—and the evening had folded them together without anyone saying much.

Now he looked into the hole like he was reading the problem.

"Smells great," he said.

Brian didn't smile.

Scott took his phone out and stared at the screen a moment before he unlocked it.

A string of notifications sat there—work emails from Chicago, a calendar reminder he'd forgotten to cancel, a missed call from a number he didn't recognize. The outside world pressing in like it still had a claim.

His boss had replied to the message Scott had sent from the driveway: OK. Keep me posted. We'll cover things here.

Scott stared at the words.

He typed, Can't. Sorry. and deleted it.

Then he typed, I'll figure it out when I'm home. and deleted that too.

He locked the phone and slid it into his pocket, feeling, for a second, lighter and more trapped at the same time.

Out on the channel, the wave runner's engine rose again and fell, too clean, too confident.

Scott looked toward the sound and then back at the hole in the yard, the tools on the towel, his brothers' shoulders set in their familiar shapes.

He stepped forward and picked up the shovel without asking whose it was.

CH 22

The Table Papers

THAT EVENING, the cabin almost worked.
The table was the same one. The chairs were the same mismatched set, legs scraped, seat cushions faded. The overhead light made a yellow circle and left the corners of the room dim.

His mother set food down in the center like she was laying out tools—cornbread, a skillet of something hot, a bowl of sliced tomatoes that looked too bright. She moved without asking if anyone was hungry.

Brian washed his hands at the sink and dried them on the dish towel even though it was already damp. Julie stood beside him, drying a serving dish, saying nothing. Matt opened a beer quietly and set the empty cap on the counter like he didn't want it to ping.

His father sat at the head of the table because that was where he sat.

He held his fork in his left hand, then switched it to his right as if correcting himself.

Scott watched the switch and looked away before it could become something.

The kids sat where there was space. Jake kept his phone face up beside his plate. Emily kept hers face down. Owen kept checking his screen as if waiting for a message.

His mother said, "No phones at the table," in the same tone she used for pass me that.

Jake slid his phone into his pocket without argument. Emily didn't move. She stared at her plate as if deciding whether rules counted for her.

His mother didn't press it. She just kept serving.

For a minute, it was ordinary.

The food was good. The cornbread was hot enough to steam when it broke. Somebody laughed at something small—Matt making a joke about how the cabin always smelled like wet towels no matter what you did.

His father smiled at the sound of laughter and leaned into it as if it warmed him.

Then his mother brought the papers to the table.

She didn't lay them down like bad news. She laid them down like instructions.

"Tuesday," she said, tapping the circled date with one finger. "That's when they come back."

Brian said, "We know."

His mother nodded and kept going anyway. "If we don't have it fixed, they fine us. If we have it half-fixed, they still fine us. If we call the wrong person, they fine us. So we do it right."

Her voice stayed calm. She kept it practical.

Matt took a bite of cornbread and chewed slowly, eyes on the paper like it might start talking.

His father reached for the papers and then stopped, hand hovering.

His mother slid them an inch closer to him.

His father picked them up and turned them sideways.

He read a line, then another. His brow tightened. "This is—" he started.

No one helped him with the word.

He cleared his throat and set the papers down again as if they were hot.

"We'll take care of it," Brian said.

His father nodded hard. "Good," he said, relieved to have something settled. He took a bite of tomato and chewed like it was work.

Scott ate slowly and listened to the room.

The ceiling fan clicked once per turn. The kids' forks scraped plates. A boat passed in the channel outside and the low engine note drifted through the screen like a memory of noise.

His mother said, "We need to talk about money."

Brian kept eating. Matt set his fork down.

"How much?" Matt asked.

His mother gave a number.

It wasn't huge. It wasn't small. It landed on the table and sat there.

Matt whistled once, then stopped himself halfway through. "That's—" he started.

"That's what it is," his mother said.

His father looked up. "How much?" he asked, as if the number had slipped past him.

His mother said it again, slower.

His father nodded, but his eyes didn't sharpen. They drifted to the window, to the dark shape of the dock outside.

Brian said, "I can cover it," and the way he said it sounded like a challenge and a gift at the same time.

Matt said, "No," quick, then softer. "We split it."

Scott didn't speak. He watched their mother's face. He watched what she didn't do—no pleading, no apology, no thank you. She let them decide because the decision was the point.

His father suddenly smiled, as if remembering something good. "Remember that year," he said, turning his fork in his fingers, "when we came down in the Corvette and your mom—"

He paused, eyes narrowing.

Scott felt his shoulders draw up.

His father said, "—your mom forgot the cooler on the driveway."

Matt laughed. "That wasn't Mom," he said.

Brian looked down at his plate.

Scott knew the story. It wasn't the cooler. It was the gas can. It was the turn onto the bluff road. It was the way his mother's hand stayed on the dash without saying a word.

His father kept smiling anyway. "Yeah," he said, nodding at his own memory as if it had been confirmed. "The cooler. We had to stop."

His mother didn't correct him.

She reached over and refilled his iced tea as if the story had gone exactly where it needed to.

Scott swallowed his next bite without tasting it.

Owen asked, "What Corvette?"

No one answered right away.

Brian said, "Old car," and the words shut the question down.

His father nodded. "Fast," he said, pleased. "Fast car."

Scott looked at his father's hands on the table. The veins stood up under the skin. The knuckles were bigger than they used to be. The hands still wanted to know what to do.

His mother said, "Eat," and started stacking plates as if the meal was already over.

Later, when the kids were outside and the kitchen was quiet except for running water, Scott stood at the sink beside his father and dried a plate.

His father washed the same fork twice.

Scott didn't say anything.

He took the fork when his father handed it to him and dried it slow, watching the water spots disappear.

Outside, the dock tapped once under the window and then again.

Farther out, a wave runner's engine rose and thinned, quick and clean, and then faded around the point.

* * *

Later, when the kitchen was quiet and the kids had been sent to bed, Linda opened the drawer under the phone and pulled out an envelope Scott had never seen.

It wasn't new. The paper was soft at the corners, creased like it had been carried around and put back again. Linda set it on the table without ceremony and smoothed it once with her palm.

Scott dried his hands on the dish towel and watched her.

"What's that," he asked.

Linda hesitated, and Scott saw the hesitation as work. "Something your dad doesn't need to see right now," she said.

Scott nodded, swallowing once.

Linda slid the flap open and pulled out a few papers folded into thirds. Old letterhead. A copy, not an original. A document with a county seal pressed into it, the kind of thing that turned a place into a legal object.

She laid it on the table and tapped a line with her finger.

Scott leaned in and read.

Earl Caldwell

He blinked. "Grandpa," he said, though it wasn't a question.

Linda nodded once. "Your dad's name isn't on it," she said. "Not the way people think it is."

Scott felt heat rise in his face. "Why," he asked.

Linda looked at him, tired. "Because Earl paid for it," she said. "Because your dad was young and proud. Because your dad didn't want help and Earl gave it anyway."

Scott stared at the name on the page and felt the cabin shift in his mind, not as a place of memory but as a thing that could be lost by paperwork.

He said, "So what does that mean."

Linda exhaled. "It means we've been getting by on everyone acting like it's simple," she said. "It means it's not."

Scott swallowed. He could hear the ceiling fan clicking again, slow and regular.

From the back room, he heard a soft noise—Rick shifting in his sleep, or waking, or dreaming.

Scott said, "Did Dad know."

Linda's mouth tightened. "He knew once," she said.

Scott felt the sentence land hard. Knew once. The way you knew a route. A knot. A story.

He said, "So what are you asking me."

Linda looked down at the papers again and then back up. "I'm asking you to help me keep it straight," she said. "I'm asking you to be the one who remembers what's on paper when your dad can't."

Scott felt the weight of it land.

He wanted to say ask Brian. Brian was the oldest. Brian was the one who made plans. Brian was the one who liked responsibility as long as it was his.

But Scott also knew why Linda asked him. Scott didn't flare up. Scott didn't leave the room. Scott stayed.

He said, "Okay."

Linda's shoulders dropped a fraction like she'd been holding them up all day.

She slid another sheet out of the envelope. A handwritten note in Earl's block letters. The ink had faded to a thinner blue.

Scott read it slowly.

It wasn't sentimental. It was instructions. Who to call. Where the deed was kept. A warning about taxes. A line about not letting the county "take it if you can help it."

Scott felt his throat tighten at the sight of his grandfather's handwriting. It made him picture Earl sitting at a table with his glasses low on his nose, writing like the cabin was a piece of equipment that needed maintenance.

Linda watched Scott read. She didn't rush him.

When he finished, Scott set the paper down carefully, as if his fingers could tear it by mistake.

He said, "Why are you showing me this now."

Linda's eyes flicked toward the hallway. "Because your dad is losing things," she said quietly. "And because Brian and Matt are going to turn it into a fight if we don't give it rails."

Scott nodded once. He didn't disagree.

He said, "So Tuesday."

Linda nodded. "Tuesday," she said. "And then after."

Scott looked at the papers again and felt the cabin become heavier in his mind, not less loved, just heavier.

He reached for the envelope and slid the documents back inside, keeping the folds the same. He closed the flap and set it back in the drawer exactly where Linda had pulled it from.

He said, "We'll do it one thing at a time."

Linda watched him, and for a second Scott thought she might reach out and touch his hand the way she had when he was a kid.

She didn't.

She only nodded and turned toward the sink, finding another dish to wash because washing was something you could finish.

Scott stood at the table a moment longer and listened to the quiet cabin.

From the living room, he could hear Brian and Matt talking low. Not arguing yet. Just the first hard edges of it, the way men started circling a subject before they admitted they were afraid of it.

Scott opened the drawer under the phone again. The envelope sat where Linda had kept it for years, soft at the corners, ordinary as a dish towel. Earl's name was still there on the page inside it, waiting.

He could have walked in and said it. Not Dad's name. Not simple. He pictured Brian stiffening, Matt flaring, the whole room turning into a vote.

He shut the drawer until it clicked.

He went back to the sink and washed a plate that was already clean, hands moving because movement was safer than speech.

Outside, the dock shifted and knocked once, softer now, the sound of the lake settling into dark.

CH 23

The Window

IN THE MORNING, with Tuesday still out in front of them, Brian wore gloves even before anyone else was fully awake.

He stood in the yard behind the cabin with a shovel planted in the dirt like a marker. The morning light was thin. Dew sat on grass and made his boots dark. The smell was there again, faint and sour, worse in the low air.

He had already made a list on the back of an envelope. A few words. A phone number. A time window—2:00 to 4:00—written beside it. The kind of list that didn't ask permission.

"They can come today," Brian said, tapping the time with his thumb. "If we miss the window, they can't get back out here before the inspection."

"We find the lid," he said, pointing with the shovel handle. "We open it. We see what we're dealing with."

Matt stood a few feet away with his hands in his pockets, sunglasses still on even though the sun hadn't cleared the trees. He looked at the disturbed soil and made a face.

"Could just call somebody," he said.

Brian didn't look up. "We are," he said. "After."

Scott held the inspection paper folded into thirds. The paper was soft from being handled. He kept it in his back pocket like it might fall out and be lost.

Their mother stood on the porch with her arms crossed, watching the yard the way she watched the lake—quiet, steady, not asking, not leaving. Julie sat on the step below her with a coffee cup between her palms, not watching the work, just present.

Their father came down the steps slower than he had yesterday. He wore a hat, brim clean, and carried a pair of work gloves in his hand like he'd brought them from somewhere else.

"What's the plan?" his father asked.

Brian answered without thinking. "Dig," he said.

Their father nodded, pleased to have a task, and stepped toward the shovel.

Brian's hand clenched the handle.

"I got it," Brian said, and it came out sharper than he meant.

Their father stopped.

For a moment, the yard went quiet except for insects.

Then, from somewhere far beyond the point, a sound started—low, sustained, like distant thunder that didn't roll away. It built and held, then roared, then cut off clean.

Their mother looked toward the water without moving. "Shootout," she said. "They moved it up the lake. Used to be you couldn't hear it from here."

Another run. The sound rose to a pitch that made the air feel tighter, then stopped.

Scott listened to the silence after. Somewhere out there, boats were running two hundred miles an hour on a three-quarter-mile course. Here, they were standing in a yard that smelled like sewage, holding shovels.

Jake's voice came from the porch. "Can we go watch?"

Scott didn't turn around. "It's twenty miles up," he said. "You'd just see a stripe."

Jake said nothing, which meant the phone was already out, searching for a livestream.

Brian put his boot on the shovel blade as if the sound didn't exist.

Scott said, "Dad, can you get the extension cord? For the pump."

Their father brightened. "Yeah," he said, and turned toward the shed with purpose.

Brian exhaled through his nose and put his boot on the shovel blade.

The first cut into the ground went easy. The dirt was soft from recent rain. The second hit something hard and the shovel rang.

"Rock," Matt said, like it was helpful.

Brian kept digging.

* * *

By midmorning, the hole was deep enough that Brian's shoulders glistened with sweat through his shirt.

He worked like he always did, turning labor into control—measured shovelfuls, dirt piled in one place, tools kept on the towel so no one stepped on them.

Scott knelt and pulled roots aside with his bare hands, careful. Matt wandered to the edge of the yard, then back, then away again, like he couldn't decide whether watching counted as helping.

The kids drifted in and out of the yard with their phones in their hands. Jake filmed the hole once and then stopped when Brian looked up.

"Don't," Brian said.

Jake shoved the phone back into his pocket, cheeks hot.

Brian found the lid by feel before he saw it. A circular edge buried under dirt, slick with mud. He scraped around it with the shovel tip, then got down on one knee and brushed soil away with gloved hands.

"There," he said.

His mother came off the porch and stood beside them without speaking.

Matt whistled low. "That's it?"

Brian didn't answer. He wedged the shovel under the edge and pried. The lid gave a little, then stuck.

"Give me the bar," he said.

Scott handed it over immediately.

Brian set his feet and pulled. The lid lifted with a wet sound that made Scott's gut clench. A stronger smell rose up, not explosive, just heavy and undeniable.

Matt stepped back.

Their mother didn't.

Brian leaned over and looked inside. His face stayed flat, but his eyes narrowed, counting.

"It's backed up," he said.

"No kidding," Matt muttered.

Brian ignored him. He pointed with the bar toward a pipe mouth visible under the rim. "That line's not moving," he said. "We clear it or we're done."

Scott said, "How?"

Brian wiped his glove on his thigh and reached for the pump.

He worked without ceremony. Hoses connected. A clamp tightened. The extension cord came from the shed and lay across the yard like a boundary.

Their father returned carrying the cord and a second pair of gloves, proud of himself. He stopped short when he saw the open tank.

He didn't react big. He only swallowed once.

Brian didn't look at his face. "Set it there," he said, pointing to the towel.

Their father placed the cord down carefully as if it could spill.

The pump whined when Brian switched it on. The sound was sharp and steady. For a moment nothing changed. Then the water in the tank shifted, a slow current starting where there had been none.

Brian leaned in, watching.

"It's moving," Scott said, surprised.

Brian nodded once. A small competence win. You could see it land in his shoulders.

He shut the pump off after a minute and listened to the silence afterward, as if the quiet could tell him whether it had worked.

Matt said, "So we're good?"

Brian didn't answer right away. He stared down into the tank and then looked toward the yard where the line ran under grass.

"Not yet," he said.

* * *

In the afternoon, the sun cleared the trees and the smell rose with the heat.

Brian wiped his face on his sleeve and looked at his list again, letters smeared from sweat.

Scott's phone rang with a number he didn't recognize.

He almost ignored it. Unknown numbers were usually spam or work. Both felt like lies today.

It rang again.

He answered. "Hello?"

A man's voice came through the line with road noise behind it. "This Scott?" the man asked.

Scott glanced at Brian. "Yeah."

"This is Randy," the voice said. "Septic. I'm by the split with the guardrail. GPS keeps telling me I'm done but I'm not seein' a driveway."

Scott's stomach dropped. He looked down the road through the trees. You couldn't see the split from here. You could feel how the roads confused people who didn't live on them.

Brian said, without asking, "Who is it?"

Scott covered the phone and said, "Pumper."

Brian's eyes sharpened. He wiped both hands on his jeans, then realized they were still dirty and stopped. "Tell him come on," he said.

Scott said into the phone, "You've got the right area. You on Horseshoe Bend Road?"

"I got a sign," the man said. "I got water on my left and a boat storage billboard. I don't got a driveway I can swing this thing into. I'm on a schedule."

Scott looked at the time on the cracked screen.

1:47

He could feel the window on Brian's envelope like a weight. Two to four. As if time obeyed paper.

Scott said, "Hold tight. I'll come get you."

Brian's head snapped up. "No," he said.

Scott didn't argue the word. He only looked at him. "If he leaves, it's not Tuesday," he said. "It's fines."

Brian's jaw worked once. He didn't like being made to choose. He liked deciding. "Go," he said finally. "Fast."

Scott turned toward the house for his keys.

Linda was already at the screen door, watching him cross the yard. She didn't ask what the call was. She read it on his face.

"The truck can't find it," Scott said.

Linda nodded once. "Take my car," she said. "Yours is blocked in."

Scott took the keys from her hand and felt the heat of her palm still on the metal.

Behind him, Jake said, "Where are you going?"

Scott didn't turn his head. "To get the septic guy," he said. "Stay here."

Jake's voice sharpened. "Why do you have to go?"

Scott heard himself inhale. He kept walking. "Because if I don't, he leaves," he said. "Stay here."

He saw Linda's eyes flick to Jake—warning and apology in one glance. Then she looked past the kids to Rick, who stood on the porch with his hat on and work gloves in his hand, watching the yard as if the hole might tell him what year it was.

Scott got in Linda's car and backed out carefully, tires crunching. The road out of Horseshoe Bend was narrow and shaded. The guardrail showed up in short bright flashes through trees.

At the split, the septic truck was parked half on the shoulder, hazard lights blinking. It was bigger up close than it had been in Scott's mind—tank and hoses and grime baked into metal. The driver stood with his phone in his hand, squinting at the map like it had insulted him.

Scott pulled up and rolled the window down.

The man looked at him and exhaled. "You Scott," he said, not a question.

Scott nodded. "Follow me," he said.

The truck swung wide behind him. It took the turn like it was dragging the road with it.

Scott drove slower than he wanted to. He watched the mirrors constantly, watching the tank clear trees, watching the tires stay on pavement. He felt his shoulders lock up. Every time the truck brake hissed behind him he imagined a mailbox crushed, a bumper clipped, the whole day turning into a new problem.

When they reached the cabin, Brian was already in the yard with the lid open and the smell sitting over it like a held breath.

The septic man stepped out and took one look down into the tank. He made a small sound that wasn't surprise. It was experience.

"All right," he said. "Keep the kids back."

Scott turned and saw Jake already halfway down the steps, phone in his hand, curiosity pulling him toward the hole like a rope.

"Jake," Scott said.

Jake stopped, offended. "What?"

Scott heard his own voice come out sharper than he meant. "Back up. It's septic."

Jake stared at him like he'd been slapped. Emily's eyes narrowed. Owen didn't look up from his screen, which made Scott angrier for no reason.

Linda stepped between them without stepping between them. "Go sit," she said, and the kids moved because her voice carried a different weight.

Rick took one step toward the open tank and stopped.

"Don't," Linda said, without looking at him.

Rick frowned as if she'd corrected him about something small. He turned away and went to the dock steps instead, keys still in his pocket, hat brim low.

Scott started after him.

Brian's voice came sharp behind him. "Scott."

Scott turned.

Brian's eyes flicked to the septic man already uncoiling a hose. "We need you here," Brian said, and Scott heard the truth underneath it: he didn't want to handle Dad. He didn't want to handle kids. He wanted to handle a problem with tools.

Scott held Brian's gaze for a beat and felt the choice bite down on him.

He went to the dock anyway.

Rick was halfway down, one hand on the rail, moving slow but sure. He stared out at the channel like he could see the line under the yard from here if he looked hard enough.

"Dad," Scott said.

Rick didn't turn. "We should check the rope," he said.

Scott stepped onto the dock and put his hand on the cleat. The rope was tight. The knot held.

"It's good," Scott said.

Rick's brow furrowed. "No," he said, and the word had conviction without content. "It's—" He stopped, searching.

Scott didn't fill the blank. He couldn't. He only said, "It's good," again, and felt the lie inside the repetition: it wasn't good. The rope was good.

Behind them, the septic hose coughed once as the pump started. A wet mechanical sound. The yard became work.

Rick looked back toward the cabin, unsettled by the noise. "What are they doing," he asked.

"Fixing it," Scott said.

Rick's face stiffened. "I could do it," he said, and the sentence came out like a complaint.

Scott's jaw worked once. He swallowed it down. "I know," he said.

He guided Rick back up the steps with his body instead of his hands, walking close enough that Rick followed without noticing he was being steered.

In the yard, the septic man wiped his hands on a rag and said, "I can pump you out. That buys you time."

Brian stared at him. "We need it clear," he said.

The man shrugged. "Clear's different," he said. "You got roots, you got a crushed line, you got a blockage down the run—pumping don't fix that. It just keeps it from backing up while you figure out who's gonna jet it."

Brian's mouth pressed flat.

The man looked at Scott, not Brian, as if Scott was the one whose answer mattered. "You want me to pump it or you want me to leave," he asked.

Scott looked at the clock in his head—Tuesday, then fines, then a mother who didn't ask for help, only said she needed it.

He nodded once. "Pump it," he said.

Brian didn't argue. He turned away and picked up the shovel again, hands needing a job.

Scott watched the hose run and felt the afternoon narrow into a smaller window: keep the man here, keep Dad off the dock, keep the kids away from the neighbor's wave runner, keep Brian from snapping at everyone until it broke something that couldn't be fixed with parts.

He didn't know which failure would cost more.

"We need a pro," Brian said finally, and it sounded like a concession.

Matt lifted his chin. "I can call a guy I know," he said, eager to contribute in a way that didn't involve dirt.

Brian's jaw set. "No," he said. "We call someone who answers and shows up."

Matt's smile faltered. "It's the same thing."

Scott lifted his hand, palm out, small. "We can call both," he said. "See who picks up."

Brian looked at him as if weighing whether compromise counted as weakness.

Their father stood near the porch rail with the work gloves still in his hand. He wasn't wearing them. He kept turning them over, fingers tracing the seams.

"I can do it," his father said suddenly.

All three brothers turned toward him.

His father looked at the shovel like it was an old friend he couldn't remember the name of. "I've done it before," he said.

Brian's face went still. "I know," he said.

His father stepped forward, eyes on the hole. He put one foot near the edge and leaned to look down.

Scott felt his muscles brace, ready to reach out.

His mother said, from behind them, "Don't get too close."

It wasn't sharp. It was enough.

His father stopped. He looked at her, then at the hole again, as if he couldn't decide which instruction mattered more.

Brian picked up the shovel and started digging again, not because digging was the next step, but because it gave his hands something to do.

Matt turned away and pulled his phone out, already dialing.

Scott watched them all move into their roles without a vote.

In the yard, the hole stayed open, lid tipped to the side, the smell sitting over it in the heat.

* * *

By late afternoon, Brian said, "We need parts," like it was a surrender.

He stood in the yard with his list in his hand, sweat drying into salt on his temples. The air above the open tank shimmered slightly. Flies circled, lazy and insistent.

Matt lifted his chin. "There's a place on the Strip," he said. "Hardware. Or we could just go to Lowe's in town."

Brian looked at him like the Strip was an insult. "We're not going to the Strip," he said.

Matt spread his hands. "It's a road," he said.

Scott said, "We can go to the hardware store by the bridge," because the sentence was neutral and neutral was his job.

Brian nodded once, already moving. "You drive," he said to Scott.

Scott didn't argue.

They left Linda at the cabin with the kids and Rick, the open hole behind the shed like a wound nobody wanted to look at for too long.

In Scott's car, Brian sat in the passenger seat with the list on his knee. Matt sat in back, restless.

At a stoplight, Brian ignored a call and turned his phone face down.

Matt saw it. "Who was that," he asked.

"Nothing," Brian said, and stared out the window.

They crossed the bridge and the Strip crowded in on the right—signs stacked, jet skis on trailers, people in swimwear like it was a uniform.

They turned off before the densest part of it, into a smaller lot with a hardware store sign sun-faded at the edges. Inside, it smelled like fertilizer, rubber, and old wood. The air was cooler. A bell above the door made a tired sound when they entered.

An older man behind the counter looked up and smiled the way locals did when they recognized a face, even if they couldn't place it.

"What can I do you for," the man said.

Brian set the list on the counter and pointed at the words as if naming them would make them real. "Septic," he said.

The man's smile flattened. "What'd it do," he asked, as calm as if Brian had said lawn mower.

Brian described it in clipped sentences. Smell. Backup. Inspection Tuesday.

The man nodded along, not surprised.

"You got a pumper coming," he asked.

Brian hesitated. "Today," he said. "Two to four, if we're ready. If we're not, it's not Tuesday they come back. It's Wednesday."

The man looked at him, eyes narrowing just slightly, not judgment, just math. "You need one," he said.

Matt said, "We know."

The man turned his attention to Scott. "Who's inspectin'," he asked.

Scott blinked. "County," he said.

The man nodded like that was enough. He reached under the counter and pulled out a spiral notebook, flipped to a page, and slid it toward Brian.

"Call these," he said, tapping two names written in block letters. "First one's mean but he shows up. Second one's slower but he'll talk to you like a human."

Brian stared at the names like they were permission.

Scott watched Brian's shoulders ease a fraction, the way they did when a plan got smaller.

Matt said, "We still need parts," impatient.

The man raised an eyebrow. "Parts ain't gonna fix a line full of roots," he said, then waved a hand toward the aisles. "But go on."

Scott walked with Brian through narrow aisles of fittings and clamps. Brian picked up a coupling, turned it over, put it back. He picked up another and held it too long, eyes unfocused.

Scott said, "What are you thinking?"

Brian's mouth pressed flat. "If I had come down sooner," he said, and stopped.

They bought more than they needed because buying something felt like doing something.

At the register, the man rang them up without hurry. When he handed Brian the receipt, he said, "It's gonna be all right," as if he were talking about more than sewage.

Brian nodded without looking up.

Back in the car, Matt said, "We should eat," like food would fix the day.

Scott's stomach turned at the thought of grease in the heat, but he nodded anyway because it kept them moving.

They pulled into a barbecue place tucked back from the Strip. The smell hit them before they shut the doors—smoke, meat, onions.

They ate near the window. Brian picked at his food like he couldn't taste it. Matt ate fast, then slower.

Outside, traffic rolled past—boats on trailers, kids with sunburned shoulders—summer moving on as if their yard didn't have a hole in it.

Matt said, mouth full, "You ever think about selling it?"

Brian looked up sharply. "No."

Matt swallowed. "We can't keep doing this," he said, and the sentence sounded like it had been waiting in him.

Brian's eyes held on him. "Doing what," he asked.

Matt glanced toward the window. Toward the lake they couldn't see from here. "Pretending Mom's fine," he said.

Scott swallowed against the ache in his chest.

Brian looked down at his plate. "We're not pretending," he said, and Scott heard how much effort it took to keep his voice flat.

Matt stared at him. "Then say it," he said.

Brian didn't.

Scott watched their hands on the table—Brian's fingers tight around a napkin, Matt's thumb worrying the edge of his napkin.

Scott said, "Let's get back," because the hole was waiting and because talking in a barbecue place felt too exposed.

Brian nodded quickly, grateful for the exit. Matt pushed his chair back, annoyed.

They walked out into hot air and sunlight that felt too bright after the dim room.

Scott drove back toward Horseshoe Bend with the smell of smoke in his clothes and the hardware store receipt on the dashboard, fluttering slightly each time the air conditioner cut on and off.

At the cabin, the septic truck was gone. The yard looked churned. The lid sat back on the tank at a slight angle, not sealed, a small failure waiting to become a bigger one.

Linda met them on the porch with her hands wet from the sink.

Brian got out before Scott had cut the engine all the way. He unfolded the page the hardware man had slid across the counter and stared at the two names as if they were a door he hadn't noticed before.

He dialed the first number and put the phone to his ear.

CH 24

Life Jackets

THAT MORNING, with the inspection due later, Scott found his mother at the screen door, watching the dock before she did anything else.

She stood at the screen door with her coffee in both hands and looked out toward the waterline like she was taking attendance. Not just the kids. The boards. The cleat. The rope. The gap under the dock where the floats hung dark and sealed.

Scott came up behind her and waited. He didn't want to break the spell of her looking.

Outside, the kids were already down on the dock, barefoot, moving without permission the way kids moved when they believed adults were occupied by adult problems.

Jake leaned over the edge to look into the water. Emily held her phone out over the boards, filming nothing in particular. Owen sat cross-legged near the steps, earbuds in, head bobbing slightly.

His mother said, without turning around, "Tell them to stay off the end."

Scott nodded and stepped onto the porch.

Before he could say anything, his father appeared behind him, already dressed, hat on, keys in his hand.

"Where's the life jackets?" his father asked.

Scott paused. "In the bench," he said, pointing at the storage seat by the porch rail.

His father stared at the bench as if it wasn't what he'd thought it was. "No," he said, and then stopped, mouth working.

His mother stepped out and set her coffee down on the porch rail. "They're in there," she said, gentle, and lifted the bench lid herself.

Bright orange vests lay folded inside.

His father nodded too hard, embarrassed by the certainty in her hands. He reached in and pulled one out, then another.

He started down the steps to the dock.

Scott followed a few steps behind, watching his father's feet find the boards.

"Hey," his father called to the kids, voice louder than it needed to be. "Life jackets."

Jake looked up, face flat. "We're on the dock."

"Life jackets," his father said again, holding the vests out like proof.

Jake stood and crossed his arms. "Grandpa, I'm fifteen. I can swim better than half the people on this lake."

Owen pulled one earbud out and watched, curious whether this would work.

His father's face tightened, not with anger but with something older. "I don't care if you swim like a fish," he said. "You wear it."

Jake looked at Scott, expecting backup, expecting the reasonable adult to intervene.

Scott didn't move.

Emily sighed and reached for a vest, rolling her eyes as she took it. "Just put it on," she said to Jake, voice low. "It's not worth it."

"It's stupid," Jake said, but his voice had shifted. He'd seen something in his grandfather's face—urgency that didn't match the situation, a tightness around the eyes that made the request feel like something else.

He took the vest and put it on wrong, arms through the neck hole, half-mocking.

"Not like that," his father said, and reached for him.

His hands hesitated in the air.

Jake stood still, the joke draining out of him.

His father's fingers found the zipper and then stopped, as if he couldn't remember which way it went.

Scott stepped closer and took the vest gently from his father's hands. "Here," he said.

He zipped it up with one quick motion and tightened the straps.

Jake let him, face unreadable now. Whatever complaint he'd been building had gone quiet.

His father watched Scott's hands work and smiled like he'd taught him that.

"There," his father said, approving. "That's right."

Scott didn't correct him.

Emily buckled her vest with practiced speed, watching her grandfather's face the way she watched screens—looking for information she hadn't been given. Owen put his on without being asked, earbuds back in, choosing silence over argument.

His father nodded at her and then looked toward the cleat, eyes narrowing.

He walked to the rope and put his hand on the knot, the same knot he'd looked at yesterday.

He tugged it once.

Then again.

He started to retie it, fingers moving fast at first and then slowing, as if the rope had changed texture. The loop went wrong. The knot tightened in the wrong place.

He frowned.

Scott watched his father's hands and felt something shift in his own chest, small and heavy.

His father tried again, and the rope slipped.

Scott reached out and caught the loose end before it fell into the water.

His father looked at him, startled, then nodded as if that had been the plan.

"Good catch," his father said.

Scott held the rope and waited.

His mother stood at the top of the steps, watching all of it without moving.

Out on the channel, a wave runner passed, engine pitched high, and the dock lifted slightly with the wake.

Tyler again—standing up, cutting the machine hard as if the water were empty.

Jake laughed and ran toward the end.

"Hey," Scott said, sharp, and Jake stopped.

Scott looked down at the rope in his hand.

He retied the knot the way his father used to, the way his own hands remembered without asking.

He pulled it tight once.

His father watched, then looked away, as if the sight asked something of him.

Scott tucked the rope end where it wouldn't trip anyone and stepped back.

His mother picked up her coffee again and turned toward the cabin.

The day had barely started, and already the roles were in place.

* * *

By midmorning the sun had burned the damp off the boards.

The dock sounded different when it dried—hollower, more certain. The kids drifted back toward the porch, life jackets unzipped, sneakers leaving wet prints on the steps.

Linda had opened windows. The cabin smelled like coffee and dish soap and lake air pulled through screens. Brian and Matt were out back with the pump tech, voices low, Julie watching from the porch with her arms crossed.

Scott stood at the sink rinsing mugs when he heard the wave runner again, closer this time, engine rising and falling like a child's laughter.

He looked out through the screen.

Tyler cut the machine hard at the mouth of their cove and let the wake roll in behind him. He stood up on the seat for a second, showing off, then dropped back down and throttled toward his dock.

Jake watched from the porch rail, eyes bright.

Emily watched too, but her face stayed flat. She already looked like she'd decided what she thought of Tyler. Scott couldn't tell if it was respect or boredom.

Owen didn't look up. Music leaked faintly from his earbuds.

Jake turned and said, "Can we?"

Scott said, "No."

It came out too fast. Too clean.

Jake's eyebrows lifted. "Why not?"

Scott set the mug in the drying rack and wiped his hands on the dish towel. He felt the old reflex—the one from childhood—to give a rule and let it stand because rules were safer than reasons.

But Jake wasn't ten. Jake knew how to ask.

Scott said, "Because that channel's not a yard." He nodded toward the water. "People drink all day and then they run those boats like they're late for something."

Jake made a face. "It's daytime."

Scott heard himself inhale and hold it.

Linda's voice came from the table behind him. "Day or night," she said, and the sentence had weight. "You don't go out there unless an adult says yes."

Jake looked at her. "Why?"

Linda didn't look away. "Because you're not strong enough to pull someone up if they go under," she said. "And because the lake doesn't care how old you are."

Scott watched Jake's face change. Not into fear. Into the kind of attention kids gave when they sensed adults were telling the truth.

Emily said, "We can swim."

Linda nodded. "I know you can," she said. "That's not the same thing."

Outside, Tyler tied up. He jumped onto his dock and ran up the steps two at a time like the day had no gravity.

He waved when he saw them on the porch. "Hey!" he called.

Jake lifted his hand halfway. Emily didn't.

Tyler pointed back toward the wave runner. "You guys wanna come ride?" he called, like offering a toy.

Jake's head snapped to Scott.

Scott didn't answer Tyler right away. He looked past him, out at the channel. A pontoon went by slow and wide, a man standing at the helm with a beer can in his hand. Music thumped from its speakers, low and steady.

Scott heard, not memory but knowledge, the way wakes stacked at night and turned into walls for a small boat.

He stepped onto the porch. "Not today," he called back, loud enough.

Tyler shrugged like it didn't matter. "Later then," he shouted, already turning away.

Jake's shoulders dropped. "You didn't even ask," he said to Scott, voice tight.

Scott felt the complaint land where it always landed—in the spot where he still wanted his mother to back him up, and still wanted not to need it.

He said, "I did ask," but it wasn't true and they both knew it.

Linda came to the screen door and held it open with her hip. "Scott," she said, not a scold. Just his name, a reminder.

Scott said, "We've got stuff to do," to Jake, and heard how weak it sounded.

Jake said, "What stuff?"

Scott stared at him and realized he didn't have a list. He had a feeling—pressure, duty, the sense that if you kept moving you could outrun whatever was coming.

He said, "Cabin stuff."

Jake laughed once, sharp. "The cabin doesn't even want us."

Emily's mouth twitched like she might smile. Owen finally looked up, one earbud pulled out.

From the living room, Rick's voice rose. "Who's at the dock?" he called, as if it were still 1976 and strangers had to be watched.

Scott went inside.

Rick stood in the doorway to the back room with a screwdriver in his hand, brow furrowed. He looked like he'd been in the middle of a job and lost the thread.

"That boy," Rick said, pointing vaguely toward the water. "He shouldn't be doing that."

Scott nodded. "I know."

Rick stared at Scott a moment, then his face shifted, softening. "You remember when Brian tried to stand up on the bow?" he asked, and the question came out too eager, like he'd found the right file in his mind and wanted to use it before it closed again.

Scott's throat tightened.

"Yeah," he said, though he didn't know which memory his father meant. There were too many.

Rick smiled at that. "Almost went in," he said, satisfied.

Linda came behind them and touched Rick's arm lightly, steering him back toward the table with the smallest pressure. "Let's eat something," she said.

Rick let her.

Jake stood in the kitchen doorway watching the adults move around each other, watching Scott follow.

Jake said, quieter now, "So what am I supposed to do?"

Scott looked at him and tried to answer honestly without making it a speech.

He said, "Stay where I can see you."

Jake's eyes narrowed. "Like a dog."

Scott felt anger rise and then stop. He remembered being twelve and hating the way safety felt like being owned.

He said, "Like a kid," and the words sounded thin.

Emily stepped past Jake and opened the fridge, looking for something as if none of it mattered.

Owen went back outside.

Scott stood at the counter with his hands flat on the laminate and listened to the wave runner's engine fade out toward the main channel again.

He didn't know if he'd protected the kids or just taught them how little their questions could move him.

CH 25

Around the Point

THAT AFTERNOON, Matt heard the cliffs before anyone said the word.

He heard it in the way Brian's voice went tight when the kids talked about going somewhere they could film. He heard it in the way Scott stopped moving for a second, then started again like he hadn't.

They were in the yard behind the cabin, the shovel still leaning against the porch post, the ground still disturbed where Brian had dug. The inspection paper was folded into thirds and sitting under a coffee mug on the table, weighted down like it might blow away.

The kids were bored in the way kids got bored now—with screens in their hands and nowhere to spend them.

Jake stood with his phone out, showing a map view, pinching and zooming. Emily leaned against the rail and watched without interest. Owen sat on the porch step and scrolled, thumb moving fast.

"We could go over there," Jake said, pointing his phone at the water like it could indicate distance. "It's not far."

"Over where?" Linda asked from the kitchen doorway.

No one answered her directly.

Brian looked up from the hole and said, "No."

It was too fast.

Matt watched him for the half second after he said it—jaw set, eyes already elsewhere—as if he'd thrown the word like a tool.

Jake blinked. "Why?"

Brian didn't look at him. He wiped his glove on his thigh. "Because the point hides you," he said. "And the channel's full."

Owen laughed once, a small sound, then stopped when nobody else joined in.

Scott said, "What are you talking about?"

Jake tilted his phone toward him. "The cliffs," he said, like it was obvious. "Dad said you used to jump."

The air changed.

Matt felt it in his shoulders, a small tightening he couldn't stop. His eyes went to the lake without deciding to. The channel was bright beyond the trees. You couldn't see the cliffs from here, but you could feel where they were on the map of the lake.

Brian said, "No I didn't."

It wasn't an explanation. It was a correction.

Emily looked up then, sharp, like she'd been waiting for something real.

Linda stepped out onto the porch. She held her coffee and didn't drink it. She said, "You're not going over there."

Jake said, "We're not going in the water."

Brian finally looked at him. "That's not the point," he said.

Matt heard himself speak before he decided to.

"It's open water and it's busy," he said. "You can't tell what's under you. You can't tell who's in the way. If something happens, we can't get to you fast."

Jake stared at him like he was testing whether that was a real reason or just adult noise.

Owen said, without looking up from his screen, "We could take a wave runner."

Brian's head snapped toward him. "Absolutely not."

Matt watched his kid's face stay blank, the way kids' faces stayed blank when they wanted to look unaffected.

Out on the channel, a wave runner went by, the engine note high and sharp. It threw a wake that the dock would feel a few seconds later.

Scott said, "They don't even have one."

Jake shrugged. "Tyler does," he said, meaning the kid two cabins down, the one with the glossy machine and no adults in sight.

Matt's gut clenched.

Linda said, "No. Not on a wave runner. Not on Tyler's."

She didn't raise her voice. The words landed anyway.

Brian went back to the hole, back turned, as if the conversation was finished.

Matt stood still and watched his kid slide his phone into his pocket with a small, practiced motion.

He didn't like how quickly the motion looked like agreement.

* * *

Later, the day slipped its leash, the way things had always happened at the lake—quietly, while adults believed they were busy.

Matt was inside in the kitchen rinsing a plate when he heard the whine of a wave runner lift up close to their cove and then move away, fast.

He stepped onto the porch and looked toward the dock.

Jake, Owen, and Emily were gone.

The dock was empty, boards hot in the sun. A pair of sandals sat kicked off near the steps.

Matt went down the steps two at a time, then slowed at the dock like running would make it worse by naming it.

The dock lifted under his feet as a wake arrived and slid under it. The boards tapped once against the floats. The sound went up his legs.

He unlocked his phone.

No messages.

Out on the channel, the wave runner sound rose high and clean and then thinned, heading away.

He walked back toward the yard behind the cabin.

Brian was bent over the hole with a wrench, shoulders tight. Scott was kneeling in the dirt, hands dark with soil. Linda stood at the porch post watching the yard like she was holding the whole day steady.

Matt said, "They took off."

Brian looked up. "Who?"

Matt nodded toward the dock. He didn't say their names. He didn't have to.

Brian's face went still. He wiped his hands on his jeans, slow. "I told him," he said.

Linda didn't move. She only said, "Go get them."

Matt started to say we don't have a boat ready, or the water's busy, or they have phones. Instead he nodded.

Brian said, "I'll go."

Scott said, "No," at the same time, and then stopped, as if the word had slipped out on its own.

Brian looked at him.

Scott's face didn't change. "I'll go with him," he said.

Matt's breath snagged. He didn't want to be the one left behind. He didn't want to be the one who didn't go.

"I'm going," he said.

No one argued.

* * *

Scott had the boat keys in his hand before Matt saw him grab them.

Brian yanked the dock rope loose and shoved the bow out. Matt stepped in hard enough to make the hull rock. The engine caught on the second turn and settled into a steady sound.

They ran out of the cove and into the channel, scanning ahead. The sun made the water bright and flat, and that brightness made distance lie.

They could hear the cliffs before they could see them—music flattened against rock, engines revving in bursts, the sound of people shouting to each other across water like it was a game.

Tyler's wave runner was there first, idling near the cluster of boats. He stood up on it, one hand on the handlebar, chin lifted like he owned the day.

Jake and Owen were in another boat's shadow, hanging onto a swim ladder with their life jackets on, eyes fixed upward. Emily stood on a low ledge with her phone out, the screen flashing in the sun as she tried to keep something in frame.

Matt's mouth went dry.

Brian said, not loud, "Get them," and started easing the boat in.

Scott held the wheel steady, threading through wakes that slapped and crossed. Matt stood at the bow with his hand on the rail, watching for the quickest way to the rocks, already feeling his legs prepare.

On the ledge above, Tyler was climbing.

He moved fast, bare feet on pale limestone, hands finding holds that weren't meant to be holds. Someone up there yelled, "Do it!" and laughed.

Tyler looked down once, grinning like it was a dare he'd already won.

Matt opened his mouth to shout and nothing came out clean.

Tyler ran two steps and launched.

For half a second his body hung against the bright sky like it belonged there.

Then he turned slightly in the air, not enough to correct, just enough to make it wrong.

He hit the water flat.

Not a clean splash. A slap, heavy and final. The sound carried off rock and came back thin.

The water swallowed him and closed.

A second passed. Then another.

Tyler didn't come up.

"Tyler!" someone yelled from above, and the laugh in the voice was gone.

Jake's face went white. He started climbing the ladder without knowing what he was doing, hands slipping on wet metal.

"Stay," Matt said, too sharp, and grabbed the back of his life jacket to hold him in place.

Brian didn't wait.

He swung himself over the side and hit the water hard, clothes and shoes dragging him down for a moment before he kicked free. He disappeared into chop and glare.

Scott cut the engine and let momentum carry them. The boat drifted. The wake made it lift and slap, lift and slap, like it was impatient.

Matt leaned over the rail and searched the surface for any sign—bubbles, an arm, anything that wasn't just wave.

Boats edged closer. People shouted from above, voices breaking as they tried to point.

Matt heard his own voice finally. "Call 911," he said to nobody, and then louder, to Emily, "Emily—call."

Emily's phone was already at her ear. Her eyes were wide and steady. She nodded once without speaking.

Brian came up farther out than Matt expected, gasping. He turned in a circle like he'd lost his bearings.

He went under again.

When he surfaced this time, he had Tyler under his arm.

Tyler's head lolled. His mouth hung open. Water streamed out of his hair and down his face like it was still trying to pull him under.

"Here!" Matt shouted, and didn't recognize the sound he made.

Scott gunned the engine just enough to close distance, careful not to make a wake that would push them apart. He killed it again and grabbed the boat hook, hands quick and sure.

Brian reached them at the same time, face blank with effort, and pushed Tyler toward the boat.

They hauled him in over the gunwale with clumsy speed—Scott bracing, Matt under Tyler's ribs, Brian pushing from below. Tyler hit the boat floor heavy and stayed there.

He didn't cough.

His chest didn't move.

Matt dropped to his knees beside him and pressed two fingers to Tyler's neck the way he'd seen someone do on television, not trusting it, doing it anyway. He couldn't find the pulse cleanly. His own fingers were shaking too much.

Brian shoved wet hair back from Tyler's forehead and pinched his nose shut.

"Come on," Brian said, and Matt didn't know if he was saying it to Tyler or to himself.

Brian gave one breath, then another, watching the chest rise like it was a miracle that had to be earned.

Tyler stayed limp.

Matt heard Jake make a small sound behind him, and the sound went through his ribs like a hook.

Brian thumped Tyler's back again and rolled him harder onto his side. Water ran out of Tyler's mouth and onto the floor, darkening the scuffed fiberglass.

For a second nothing happened.

Then Tyler coughed—one ugly, tearing cough—and gagged.

Matt exhaled a breath he didn't know he'd been holding and felt his hands start to shake.

Scott said, "We're going back," and didn't ask.

Emily climbed in over the side last, phone still in her hand, screen lit with something she didn't look at.

They turned away from the cliffs with the engine low, threading back through traffic while Tyler lay on the floor coughing in wet bursts, eyes half-open and unfocused.

Jake sat rigid near the console, hands clenched, staring at Tyler like he couldn't make his brain accept that bodies could go limp.

Owen didn't look away. His face stayed blank, the way kids' faces stayed blank when they were trying not to be little.

Behind them, the cliffs kept making noise.

When they reached their dock, Linda was already halfway down the steps, phone in her hand, dish towel forgotten on the porch rail.

"What happened?" she said, and didn't wait for an answer.

They lifted Tyler between them—Scott under one arm, Matt under the other, Brian at his back—boots scraping, boards creaking, the dock tapping once under the weight.

Tyler's eyes fluttered. He tried to speak and couldn't.

Linda put her hand on his cheek, quick and sure, like she was checking a fever. Then she moved, making space, already looking down the drive for headlights.

In the yard, Tyler coughed again and curled onto his side. His chest heaved. The sound of it was loud in the quiet that followed the engine.

Someone had called it in. A siren started somewhere up the road, thin at first, then closer.

Tyler's mother came up the drive at a run a moment later, hair loose, face bare, moving like she'd been told a word and nothing else.

She dropped to her knees beside her son and put her forehead to his shoulder. Her whole body shook once. Then she steadied herself and sat up like she hadn't.

Linda reached for Jake then—both hands on his shoulders, turning him to face her the way she'd done when he was little, checking without saying numbers. When she pulled him into her, it was hard enough to hurt.

Matt watched Linda's face press into Jake's hair. Her shoulders shook once. Then she steadied herself and let go like she hadn't.

Brian said to Jake, "Give me that."

Jake hesitated. Then he held the phone out.

Brian took it and looked at the screen. The video was rock and sky and Tyler's legs, then the turn in the air. The slap of water came through the speaker small and wrong. A shout cut off halfway through.

Brian watched for a few seconds, then stopped it. His thumb hovered over the trash icon, then moved away.

Matt saw it and felt his stomach drop in a way that had nothing to do with water.

Brian locked the screen and held the phone a moment longer than he needed to.

Jake's face faltered. "What?"

Brian handed it back without meeting his eyes. "Put it away," he said. "Now."

Matt watched Scott, waiting for him to say something. Scott's face stayed blank, eyes on the dock boards, as if he'd chosen not to see.

Brian exhaled once through his nose and turned away, walking up the dock steps without looking back.

Matt stayed on the dock a second longer and watched Jake slip the phone into his pocket.

The motion was small and practiced.

It looked like nothing.

* * *

That night, the cabin kept trying to return to ordinary.

Linda made coffee no one drank. She moved dishes from one counter to another and wiped the same spot twice. The porch light stayed on even though bugs battered it without learning.

Matt sat at the kitchen table with his hands flat on the wood and listened to the house. Water running. A drawer closing. Rick's slow footsteps in the hall, stopping and starting as if the rooms had shifted.

Julie came in from the back bedroom and shut the door with a gentleness that didn't match her face.

"He won't talk," she said.

Matt didn't ask who. "Jake?"

Julie nodded once. Her hair was still damp from a rushed shower. She'd put on a clean shirt like it made her more useful. Her eyes kept drifting to the window, to the dark shape of the dock beyond it.

"He keeps saying he didn't go," she said. "Like if he says it enough it'll be true."

Matt swallowed. "He didn't jump," he said.

Julie looked at him then, sharp. "I know," she said. "I know what you mean." She exhaled hard through her nose and rubbed her thumb along the edge of her phone case until the plastic squeaked. "I'm not mad at him for being there. I'm mad at him for making me picture it."

Matt didn't have a clean reply. He understood. He also didn't want to turn it into a family argument with the lake still in everyone's mouth.

From the living room, Brian's voice rose once and fell again. Not yelling. Just the sound of a man trying to keep his sentences short enough not to break.

Julie said, quieter, "Did you see what he recorded?"

Matt felt his gut drop. "Brian did," he said. "He told him to put it away."

Julie's mouth twitched as if she might argue. Then she didn't. She set her phone down on the table and stared at it like it was something dangerous.

"My boss texted," she said.

Matt waited.

Julie picked the phone back up and turned the screen toward him for half a second. A message thread. A line that started with Can you be back... and a second line with a time attached to it. The outside world placing its claim.

She turned the screen back to herself and didn't answer it.

Matt watched her thumb hover. He saw the decision fight its way through her face.

Julie locked the phone and set it down again, face-down this time. "We're staying," she said, and the sentence sounded like she was talking to herself more than to him.

Matt nodded once. He didn't thank her. Thank you would make it bigger than she wanted it to be.

Rick appeared in the doorway, keys in his hand. He looked from Julie to Matt as if checking whether they belonged here.

"Where's your mom," Rick asked.

Matt felt something twist. "She's right here," he said, and nodded toward the kitchen as if Linda was in the next room. He wasn't sure why he did it. He only knew the word your was wrong.

Rick frowned, uncertain, and then smiled, relieved to have found something he could agree with. "Okay," he said. "Okay."

He wandered toward the porch, then stopped and looked back. "We got the boat tied," he said, proud.

Matt said, "Yeah," and felt the lie sit between his teeth.

Julie watched Rick go with her lips pressed together, eyes damp and not letting it show.

In the back bedroom, a floorboard creaked. Then another.

Julie didn't move. She only said, "I'm going to try again," and walked down the hall toward Jake.

Matt sat in the kitchen and listened to her knock once and speak softly through the door.

He couldn't hear the words.

He could hear the tone.

CH 26

Proof

BRIAN NOTICED THE WATER was lower than he remembered. That was the first thing he noticed each morning now—not the color, not the smell, but the way the shoreline had crept back and left rock and old timber exposed. The dock looked longer. The boards sounded different under his weight.

Jake crouched near the edge, intent on something small. A stick. A bug. A nail head in the wood. The precise reason didn't matter. What mattered was the way his weight shifted forward, one sneaker close to slipping on the damp plank.

"Hey," Brian said, not loudly.

Jake looked back, face flat. Not angry, exactly. Closed. He turned again without answering.

Brian stepped closer without deciding to. His body knew the distance better than his mind did. Two steps. One hand ready. He stopped himself there, fingers curling and uncurling once.

Out on the channel a wave runner went by, the engine note high and thin. The wake rolled toward their cove. The dock lifted slightly, then settled.

Jake leaned farther, testing the edge with his toes the way children did when they were learning what gravity allowed.

"Careful," Brian said.

The word came out sharper than he meant.

Jake straightened and looked at him. "I am."

He believed it. That was the problem.

Brian waited.

He counted without numbers. One breath. Another. He watched Jake's shoulders rise and fall.

Jake lost interest on his own and stood up, stick forgotten. He walked past Brian toward the steps without looking at him.

Halfway up, his phone buzzed in his pocket.

Brian heard the buzz and felt an irritation that surprised him. Not at the phone. At the way it made Jake's attention snap somewhere else instantly, as if the lake couldn't compete with a screen.

Jake pulled the phone out, glanced at it, and kept walking.

Brian said, "Who's that?"

Jake didn't stop. "Nobody."

Brian watched him go and felt his hands tighten around nothing.

He could have called him back. He could have made a rule. He could have taken the phone and held it like proof of who was in charge.

Instead he stayed where he was and let Jake go inside.

Only then did he realize he'd been holding his breath.

* * *

Later, when the sun was higher and the dock boards had warmed, Jake came back down.

He stood at the cleat and stared at the rope without touching it. The knot sat where it always sat, the tail tucked the way his grandfather used to tuck it.

"Dad," Jake said.

Brian turned. "Yeah?"

Jake didn't ask about the cliffs. He didn't say why can't we. He didn't mention what he'd filmed.

He said, "Can I go see Tyler later?"

Brian felt his gut clench.

He looked past his son toward the channel. The water was bright in the sun. The wave runner's path was easy to imagine. A straight line to trouble. A quick return. A story that could be edited afterward.

He heard his own father's voice in his head saying rules without reasons.

He looked at his son's face and saw himself at that age—chin lifted, waiting to be told no so he could hate it.

Brian said, "Not today."

Jake's eyes flashed. "Why?"

Brian swallowed.

He said, "Because I watched him go under."

Jake's face changed, quick and involuntary, like he'd thought the adults would forget it faster than he did.

Brian added, quieter, "Stay close."

Jake stared at him for a long moment like he was trying to decide whether that counted as an answer.

Finally he nodded once, too small to be agreement, and turned away.

Brian watched him go and rested his hand on the rail.

The dock shifted under his palm, faint and steady.

When he looked back out over the lake, it looked the same as it always had.

It was only his body that had changed.

* * *

After dinner, the cabin quieted the way it always did—screens vibrating faintly, someone rinsing a plate, the hum of the fridge filling the spaces where talk would have been.

Brian stood in the hallway and watched Jake at the table.

Jake's phone was in his hands, screen bright against his face. His thumbs moved fast. Not texting his mother. Not playing a game. Something tighter than that.

Brian could have let it go.

He felt the old impulse to pretend a thing wasn't happening so he wouldn't have to become the kind of father who demanded proof. He'd hated that kind of father when he was a kid. He'd learned to lie clean because of it.

But now he could see the way the light held Jake's attention, the way it cut him out of the room.

Brian said, "What are you doing?"

Jake didn't look up. "Nothing."

Brian waited.

Jake's shoulders tensed. He set the phone down face-up on the table like a dare.

The screen showed a video paused on a blurred frame of water and sky. A wave runner's bow lifting. Someone shouting off-camera. The image was shaky, too bright.

Brian felt his stomach drop. He hadn't realized it was still on a phone.

Jake said, "Everyone has it."

Brian stared at the frame until it started to feel like he was staring at a person. "That's not the point," he said.

Jake's voice sharpened. "Tyler's fine."

Brian heard the word fine the way adults used it when they were trying to make a thing small enough to carry.

He said, "He's alive."

Jake's mouth tightened at the correction.

Brian lowered his voice. "You don't keep that," he said.

Jake glanced toward the living room where Emily sat on the couch with her legs tucked under her, phone in her lap, pretending not to listen. Owen lay on the rug, headphones on, screen glowing.

Jake said, "Why?"

Brian could have given a rule without a reason.

He said, "Because it isn't yours."

Jake scoffed. "It's my video."

Brian's hands tightened around the back of a chair. "It's his day," he said. "It's his family's day. It's his mother waking up and thinking she almost didn't get him back."

Jake stared at him, and for a second Brian saw the boy he used to be—stubborn, insulted, waiting for the adults to say the real truth.

Jake said, quieter, "I didn't post it."

Brian nodded once. He believed him. That wasn't enough.

"You still have it," Brian said.

Jake's eyes flicked toward the screen again. The paused frame was almost beautiful in its accident—sun on water, a body about to vanish.

Brian said, "Delete it."

Jake didn't move.

From the kitchen, Linda's voice rose and fell, talking softly to someone—Tyler's mother, maybe, or Julie on the porch. The words didn't carry. The tone did. The tone was tired.

Jake said, "What if we need it?"

Brian said, "For what?"

Jake swallowed. "If someone says we did something," he said. "If someone blames us."

Brian felt a flash of something he didn't want to name: pride, maybe, that his son was thinking of consequences. Fear too, because it meant Jake already lived in a world where proof mattered more than truth.

Brian said, "No one's blaming you."

Jake's face stayed hard. "You don't know that."

Brian took a breath, slow, and tried to speak like a person and not a rule.

He said, "If something happens and an adult needs it, they'll ask," he said. "But you don't keep it like it's a trophy."

Jake's jaw clenched. "It's not a trophy."

Brian watched his son's thumbs hover over the screen. Hesitate.

Brian remembered being ten and seeing a dead fish float belly-up near their dock, the way he'd stared at it too long, fascinated and sick at the same time. He remembered his father's hand on the back of his neck, steering him away without explanation.

He didn't put his hand on Jake.

He said, "Do it," and kept his voice calm enough that the room wouldn't hear.

Jake stared at him for a long moment.

Then, with a sharp movement like ripping something, he tapped and held, hit delete, confirmed it. The screen went blank, then filled with a different list, empty where the video had been.

Jake's breathing changed—faster, then slower, like he hadn't known he'd been holding it.

Brian said, "Thank you."

Jake looked at him like the words were a trick.

He said, "So now what?"

Brian didn't have an answer that would satisfy him. He didn't have a speech about respect or faith or the lake being dangerous.

He said, "Now we go to bed," and heard how small it sounded.

Jake pushed his chair back, harder than necessary. He grabbed his phone and walked past Brian without looking at him.

At the doorway he stopped and said, not turning, "You're always scared."

Brian didn't answer.

He stood in the hallway and listened to Jake's footsteps fade into the back room.

In the living room, Emily lifted her eyes briefly, just long enough for Brian to see she'd heard everything.

Then she looked back down at her phone and kept her face blank, the way kids did when they didn't want adults to know they were holding something too.

CH 27

The Question

EMILY WAS ALREADY MOVING. She stood at the top of the dock steps with her hair pulled back tight, life jacket unzipped and hanging open like she'd put it on to satisfy someone and then forgotten about it. She held a towel over one shoulder. She didn't look at the water first. She looked at the hardware—cleat, rope, the place where the boards met the floats.

"Tyler's awake," she said, as if reporting weather.

Jake hovered behind her, quiet, hands in his pockets, eyes on the channel.

Brian said, "I know."

His daughter nodded once and walked down the dock without hurry. Her bare feet found the boards easily. She didn't flinch when the dock shifted under her weight. She knew the tap and lift of it. She belonged to the movement.

At the ladder, she sat and lowered herself in, controlled, not splashing. The water took her and she went under clean. When she surfaced a few yards out, she pushed wet hair off her face and treaded water like it was nothing.

"Watch," she called.

She dove again and came up farther out, strong and sure, turning her head to sight the dock before she turned back. He'd never told her to do that. She'd learned it anyway.

Jake stood near the edge and watched her with open admiration.

"She's good," Jake said.

"Yeah," Brian said.

His daughter swam back and grabbed the ladder, pulling herself up without help. Water streamed off her arms and onto the boards. She climbed past them and sat on the dock edge, breathing easy.

She looked at him then, eyes level. "You worry too much about him," she said.

He almost laughed. Almost told her she had no idea what worry felt like when it lived in your hands.

Instead he said, "He moves like he doesn't hear the water."

Emily made a face. "He's a kid."

Jake's shoulders drew up at that. He stared at his shoes.

Brian said, softer, "So are you."

She rolled her eyes like he'd said something stupid. "Not like that," she said, and stood up.

The wave runner's engine rose out on the channel and then dropped as it turned. The sound was clean and sharp, too confident.

His daughter looked toward it and lifted her chin. "Can I go see them?"

He felt something clench low in his gut.

He looked at her face. She wasn't asking to rebel. She was asking the way you asked for car keys—already moving toward yes in your body.

He looked at his son, waiting for him to complain. His son didn't. He only watched.

Brian said, "Stay where I can see you."

His daughter smiled once, quick, like she'd gotten what she wanted. "I will," she said, and ran down the dock, feet slapping boards.

* * *

Emily ran up the steps and across the yard without looking back.

Brian followed at a slower pace with Jake beside him, both of them walking like they had somewhere to be and didn't want to say what it was.

Tyler's cabin sat two doors down, porch shaded, screen door half-open. The wave runner wasn't moving. It sat up on the lift like a toy someone had lost interest in.

Tyler's mother stood on the porch with her arms folded tight across her chest. She looked up when she saw them and her face changed in a way Brian recognized—relief arriving too late to feel clean.

Emily went up the steps first and held the towel out without speaking.

Tyler was on the couch inside, wrapped in a blanket with wet hair stuck to his forehead. His skin looked pale. He coughed once, deep and ugly, then tried to swallow it down as if it was embarrassing.

Emily stepped closer and said, "Hi," like this was a normal visit.

Tyler didn't answer. His eyes moved to Jake, then to Brian, then away.

Jake stood in the doorway and didn't move.

Brian didn't know what to do with his hands.

Tyler's mother said, quietly, "They said he'll be sore. They said watch him tonight."

Linda's voice came from behind them in the yard, talking to someone on the phone, giving directions like she'd done it before.

Brian nodded once. He didn't say I'm sorry. He didn't say thank God. He only looked at Tyler's chest, the way it rose and fell, like he was counting it.

Emily turned and walked back out onto the porch as if she'd completed a task.

"You worry too much," she said again, softer now, and he couldn't tell if it was comfort or complaint.

Brian stayed on the porch a moment longer, hand resting on the rail, feeling the boards' faint vibration under his palm.

He didn't go inside.

* * *

That night, Emily found him on the dock.

Brian sat near the cleat with his feet on the boards, not hanging over. The lake was black beyond the porch lights. The channel carried sound in thin pieces—music from one of the lakeside bars, an engine throttling up and then easing down, laughter that didn't belong to anyone he knew.

Emily stepped down the dock without asking if she could. Her hair was damp again like she'd showered and then gone back outside anyway. She held her phone in one hand but didn't look at it.

She sat beside him with her knees pulled up and her arms wrapped around them, posture guarded in a way that wasn't fear. It was choice.

For a while, she didn't speak.

Brian watched the water line where he could just make out the pale edge of limestone. He could picture the cliffs across the channel without seeing them.

Emily said, finally, "Tyler's mom cried."

Brian didn't look at her. "Yeah," he said.

Emily's voice stayed flat. "She tried not to."

The sentence landed. He thought of Linda on the porch earlier, coffee in her hands like a tool. He thought of Julie inside with the kids, holding things steady while he sat out here.

Emily said, "Jake's mad at you."

Brian exhaled through his nose. "He'll get over it."

Emily turned her head and looked at him in the dark like she was taking inventory. "No he won't," she said. Not dramatic. Just certain.

Brian's jaw set. "Then he won't," he said.

Emily's mouth twitched, not a smile. "You're bad at talking," she said.

Brian almost laughed, but it didn't come. "I know."

Emily held her phone up between them, screen dark. "I have that video," she said.

Brian's stomach dropped.

He kept his voice even. "Do you."

Emily nodded once. "I started filming when Tyler climbed up there," she said. "It just... kept recording."

Brian didn't move. He felt the dock shift under him with a wake from somewhere far off.

Emily said, "I didn't send it."

Brian heard the defense and didn't blame her for it.

He said, "Delete it."

Emily stared at him. "Why."

There it was again—why, like a wedge.

Brian kept his eyes on the black water. He said, "Because it's not for you to keep."

Emily's breath came out sharp. "That's not an explanation," she said.

Brian felt heat rise in his face. Not anger. Shame, maybe. The same heat he'd felt as a boy when adults told him rules and made him pretend he understood.

He said, "Because it turns into a story that belongs to everyone," he said, and heard how close it came to being abstract. He pulled it back. "Because Tyler has to live in that body tomorrow."

Emily's fingers tightened around the phone. "He almost died," she said.

Brian said, "I know."

Emily said, "Then why is everyone acting like it didn't happen?"

Brian looked at her then.

Her face was open in the dark. Not accusing. Just young enough to believe adults should be able to name things.

Brian swallowed. "Because if we talk about it too much, it gets bigger," he said.

Emily's eyes narrowed. "It should be big," she said.

Brian didn't have an answer that would make her feel safe. He only had his own body's memory of water closing over someone's head.

Emily said, "Is that what happened to you?"

Brian felt something catch in his throat.

"No," he said too quickly.

Emily waited. She didn't look away. She didn't let him change the subject by refusing to.

Brian stared at the cleat and the rope looped around it. He could feel the roughness of the dock boards under his palm. He could smell lake water and mosquito spray and a faint trace of gasoline.

He said, quieter, "When I was your age, we saw somebody go under," he said. "Not a kid. A teenager."

Emily's eyes widened a fraction. "Here?"

Brian nodded once.

Emily's voice dropped. "Did you save him?"

Brian felt the word save snag in him. He shook his head. "No," he said.

Emily stared at him like she'd expected him to be the kind of father who saved people.

Brian said, "We didn't even know his name," and the sentence came out like a confession.

Emily looked down at her phone, thumb resting on the side button. "So you're scared all the time," she said, and it wasn't insult. It was mapping.

Brian didn't argue with it.

Emily said, "Jake thinks you don't trust him."

Brian watched a small insect hit the porch light and fall away.

He said, "I trust him," and knew it wasn't fully true.

Emily snorted softly. "No you don't."

Brian's mouth pressed flat. He said, "I trust him to be a kid," he said. "That's the problem."

Emily leaned her head back and stared up at the dark sky as if it might answer something. "We're not little," she said.

Brian said, "I know."

Emily's voice sharpened. "Then stop treating us like we are."

Brian held her gaze. He tried to speak like a person and not like a rule.

He said, "I'm not mad that you want to do things," he said. "I'm not mad that you ask why. But this lake isn't fair. It doesn't give you a second chance just because you're smart."

Emily listened, eyes steady, and Brian saw that she was old enough for the sentence to land, but still young enough to want it to protect her.

Emily looked down at her phone again.

"Okay," she said, and the word surprised him.

She tapped, held, found the video, and deleted it without drama. The screen flickered and then the file list shifted, smaller.

Brian felt a pressure release in his chest that he hadn't known was there.

Emily didn't look at him. "I still remember it," she said.

Brian nodded. "Me too," he said.

Emily said, very quietly, "Tyler's mom asked me what I saw."

Brian felt the question land. "What'd you say?"

Emily's voice stayed even. "I said he stood up," she said. "And then I said I didn't know."

Brian stared at her, surprised.

Emily looked back. "Because I don't," she said, defensive now. "I don't know why he did it."

Brian heard something in her sentence that felt like a crack of light: an admission that sometimes there wasn't a reason that made it safe.

He said, "That's honest."

Emily's shoulders dropped a fraction. "I'm tired," she said, and stood up.

She took two steps, then turned back.

"Dad," she said.

Brian looked up.

Emily hesitated, like she wasn't used to asking for what she wanted in plain words.

She said, "If you're going to say no, tell us why," she said. "Not a rule. The reason."

Brian felt the request land hard because it was fair.

He nodded once. "Okay," he said.

Emily watched him for a second, then turned and walked back up the dock, bare feet quiet on boards.

Brian stayed where he was and listened to the channel sounds thin out as the night got later.

He didn't feel calmer.

He only felt more responsible, which was close enough for now.

CH 28

The Folder

BY THEN, the cabin ran like a worksite. By late morning, the hole was open again and the smell sat in the heat, heavier as the sun rose.

Brian dug in measured cuts, back bent, jaw set. Scott knelt beside the edge and pulled roots aside, dirt packing under his fingernails. Matt hauled buckets of soil out without speaking, breathing hard, face turned away like the work didn't mean anything.

Their father came into the yard with his hat on and work gloves in his hand again.

He stood at the edge of the disturbed grass and looked down into the hole.

"That's not where it is," he said.

Brian froze.

Scott looked up.

Their father pointed a few feet to the left as if he could see the pipe through dirt. "It runs there," he said, confident.

Brian's face went still. "No," he said, too flat.

Their father frowned, offended. "I've done this," he said.

Scott stepped closer and said, "Dad, can you show me where you think it is?"

His father brightened. He pointed again, then started describing a line, his hand moving in the air like he was drawing a map.

Scott listened, nodding, letting the story have space.

Behind him, Brian started digging again, deeper, harder.

Matt hauled another bucket of dirt out and set it down with more force than he needed.

Their mother stood at the porch post and watched, coffee in her hand, eyes on the yard the way they stayed on the water.

No one said the word for what was happening to their father.

They worked around it instead.

* * *

At noon, a truck pulled into the gravel and a man got out wearing a company shirt and carrying a clipboard.

He shook hands with Brian first. Brian's handshake was too firm, too long, as if he wanted the man to understand something without words.

The man walked to the hole, looked down, and made a small sound of recognition.

"Yeah," the man said. "You got a blockage."

He said it plain. A blockage. Common. Just work.

Matt exhaled loudly through his nose, relieved to have someone else say it.

Brian asked questions fast—how much, how long, what's the worst case—and the man answered without being rushed.

Scott stood back and watched Brian's posture soften a fraction as responsibility moved from his shoulders to someone else's hands.

Matt's shoulders softened too.

For a moment, it looked almost like a family.

Then the man named a price.

Matt's face stiffened.

Brian's face didn't change at all.

The number landed, heavy and familiar.

Their mother nodded once, already deciding.

Brian said, "Do it," and the word ended the discussion.

No one argued.

The man went back to his truck to get equipment.

Matt stared at the ground and said, very softly, "I didn't mean for any of this."

Scott looked at him.

Matt didn't look up. He pressed his thumb hard against the dark screen until his knuckle went white.

Brian pretended not to hear.

Scott said, "I know."

He didn't know what else to say that wouldn't start a fight.

Matt's mouth worked like he wanted to say more and didn't know how.

He shoved his phone into his pocket and walked toward the shed to get out of sight.

Scott watched him go and then looked back at the hole, the open lid, the disturbed ground.

A breeze moved through the trees and brought the lake smell in for a second—gasoline, algae, sun on wood.

He heard, for a second, beer cans clinking in a sack.

He swallowed and went back to work, hands in dirt, keeping his eyes on what needed doing.

* * *

That night, the paperwork came out.

Linda laid it on the kitchen table in a neat stack—inspection report, invoice from the septic company, a folded estimate with numbers circled in pen. She did it the same way she laid out food when they were kids: one thing after another, no drama, no room for argument to pretend it was about something else.

Scott sat with a mug of coffee he didn't want, watching the paper edges lift slightly in the airflow from the window fan.

Brian stood at the counter with his arms folded, jaw set. Matt sat sideways in a chair with one ankle resting on the other knee, phone in his hand but screen dark, pretending he wasn't nervous.

Rick came in last and stood behind Linda's chair. He looked down at the stack as if it were mail that didn't belong to them.

"What's all that," Rick asked.

Linda didn't look up. "The septic," she said. "The inspection. The bill."

Rick frowned. "We already fixed that," he said, and the words came out with irritation, like he'd been accused of neglect.

Scott's stomach knotted.

Brian said, "Dad," and stopped. He didn't know which sentence to choose.

Linda said, gentle, "We're fixing it," and slid the top sheet toward Rick so he could see the company name.

Rick leaned forward. He squinted. He nodded once like he recognized the letters, then his face shifted away again.

"How much," he asked, already annoyed at the answer.

Linda tapped the circled number. "This much," she said.

Rick's eyes widened. "That's robbery," he said.

Matt let out a short laugh that wasn't amused. "Welcome to 2025," he said.

Brian's head snapped toward him. "Don't," he said, low.

Matt's mouth tightened. He looked away.

Rick said, louder, "We don't pay that," like his volume could rewrite it. "I'll call him."

Brian said, "He's already gone."

Rick stared at him. "Then bring him back," he said.

Silence held for a beat.

Scott watched his mother's hands. She clasped them once, then opened them again on the table like she was keeping herself from gripping the edge.

Brian spoke carefully, as if talking to a child, and Scott hated him for it even as he understood why. "Dad, it's done," Brian said. "We had to do it before Tuesday."

Rick looked at Linda, seeking confirmation.

Linda nodded. "It's done," she said.

Rick's shoulders dropped a fraction. He looked suddenly tired.

"So who pays," Matt asked, too blunt.

Brian's eyes flicked toward Scott. The old dynamic—the way decisions wanted to slide to whoever stayed calm the longest.

Scott said, "We can split it," and heard how simple it sounded.

Matt's laugh came again, this time sharper. "Split it," he repeated. "Like we're in college and ordering pizza?"

Brian's voice dropped. "What's your plan," he asked, and the question had heat now. "You got one?"

Matt's eyes flashed. "My plan is we stop pretending this place belongs to all of us if only one of us is always here," he said.

Scott felt the sentence land like a tool dropped on the floor.

Brian said, "I'm here," and the words came out too hard. "I drove fifteen hours to be here."

Matt pointed at him with his beer bottle. "You drove fifteen hours because Mom called you," he said. "Not because you love pressure washers and septic tanks."

Brian's face went blank. "You want to say I don't love the cabin," he said.

Matt said, "I want to say you love being the guy who shows up and tells everybody what to do."

Scott looked at Linda.

Her face didn't change. But her eyes shifted briefly toward the window, toward the dark yard, like she wanted out of the room for a second.

Rick said, "Enough," and his voice carried the old authority for a moment. He pointed at the papers. "We're not fighting over a bill."

Brian turned toward him. "We're not fighting over the bill," he said, and Scott heard in it the truth: they were fighting over who would carry their father's decline and what the cabin meant if he couldn't.

Rick's brows knit. "Then what," he asked, confused.

No one answered.

Linda took a breath. She slid one paper out from the stack and held it down with her palm. "We need a plan," she said.

Matt stared at her. "What kind of plan," he asked, voice smaller now.

Linda's eyes stayed on the paper. "A plan for the cabin," she said. "And a plan for your dad."

The words sat in the kitchen like smoke.

Rick shifted his weight. "I'm right here," he said, offended.

Linda reached back without looking and touched his wrist lightly, a small calming gesture that also claimed him. "I know," she said.

Scott felt his throat tighten. He wanted to protect his father from being spoken about like that. He also wanted someone to say it plainly so they could stop pretending.

Brian said, too quickly, "We don't need to decide that tonight."

Matt said, "We do," and his voice cracked on the word like surprise.

Scott looked at his brothers.

Brian's eyes were bright with anger he didn't know where to put. Matt's leg bounced under the table, the way it had when they were kids and adults were talking about money.

Scott said, "Tuesday was the inspection," he said. "We got through Tuesday."

Brian nodded, relieved to have a smaller target. "We did," he said.

Matt stared at the table. "Then what," he asked.

Rick leaned forward suddenly and picked up the estimate, holding it in both hands like it weighed too much. He squinted hard. "Earl would've known," he said.

Scott froze.

Linda's face softened, then steadied. "Earl's gone," she said gently.

Rick blinked. He looked up at her, confused, as if she'd changed the subject without warning.

Something turned in him, heavy and hot.

Brian's face broke for a second—the anger falling away into something else. He looked down at the table and picked up his phone, turning it once in his hands without unlocking it, as if the motion could keep him steady.

Matt swallowed and said, very quietly, "Jesus."

Linda reached for the estimate and slid it back into the stack. She didn't take it from Rick like a scold. She replaced it like a nurse putting tools away.

Rick let her.

Scott stood up before he knew he was going to. The chair legs scraped the floor.

Everyone looked at him.

Scott said, "I'll make a folder," he said, and the sentence sounded ridiculous, small against what was happening. But it was something his hands could do.

He opened the drawer by the phone and found an old manila folder that had once held fishing permits. He slid the papers inside, one by one, smoothing them down so the edges lined up.

When he was done, he wrote SEPTIC on the tab in block letters and set it back on the table in front of Linda.

No one thanked him.

No one stopped fighting either.

But for a moment, the papers were contained.

Outside, a wave runner passed on the channel, its engine note high and steady, and the window glass vibrated faintly with the sound.

Scott looked toward the dark yard and felt the lake pulling at all of them the way it always had—quiet, patient, waiting for someone to slip.

CH 29

Keys in the Dark

LATER THAT NIGHT, Scott heard the screen door open and close once, soft.

He was in the back room half-asleep, the cabin cooled down for the first time all day, when the sound pulled him upright. For a second he didn't know where he was. Then he smelled lake air through the screens and remembered.

He listened.

No voices. No footsteps inside.

He swung his legs over the bed and stepped into the hallway, careful not to wake anyone. The cabin was dim, porch light bleeding through the screen, the living room couch a dark shape.

The screen door clicked again.

Scott moved quietly and stepped onto the porch.

Rick was already halfway down the dock steps, hat on, keys in his hand. He moved with purpose, not stumbling, but the purpose didn't fit the hour.

"Dad," Scott said, not loud.

Rick stopped and turned his head as if surprised to find Scott there. "We need to bring it in," he said.

"Bring what in?"

Rick pointed toward the channel. In the dark, the water was a sheet. The boat sat tied up exactly where it should be.

"The boat," Rick said. "It's drifting."

Scott felt his gut clench. He looked toward the cleat. The rope was snug, knot tight.

"It's tied," Scott said.

Rick shook his head. "No," he said, and the word had conviction. "Earl told me to. He said don't leave it out when the wind changes."

Scott's breath caught.

He didn't correct the name. Not yet.

He stepped down onto the dock and walked to the cleat. He kept his movements slow, deliberate, like he was showing a child something that had to be learned by watching.

He put his hand on the rope and pulled once. The knot held.

"See," Scott said. "It's good."

Rick stared at the rope, then at the water, as if the proof didn't settle anything.

"We're gonna lose it," Rick said, and his voice cracked on the sentence like fear had gotten in.

Scott swallowed.

He said, "We won't," and tried to make it true with tone.

Rick lifted the keys in his palm as if he'd forgotten why they were there. He stared at them, then shoved them into his pocket, embarrassed.

He looked past Scott toward the dark cabin. "Your mom," he said, and stopped.

Scott waited.

Rick's mouth worked. "She'll worry," he said finally.

Scott nodded once. "I know."

Rick's eyes narrowed. "Don't tell her," he said, and the sentence sounded like a teenager's request, not a husband's.

Scott felt something twist in him. He wanted to say she's your wife. He wanted to say she already knows everything without being told.

Instead, he said, "Okay."

Rick watched him for a long moment, as if trying to decide if Scott was on his side.

Then Rick turned and walked back up the dock, slower now. Scott followed a step behind, close enough to catch him if he slipped, far enough not to touch him.

At the top of the steps, Rick stopped and looked out at the cove as if he were taking one last measurement.

"I can still drive," he said suddenly.

His breath caught. "I know you can," he said, because arguing about it here would be cruel.

Rick nodded, satisfied, and went inside.

Scott stayed on the porch a moment longer, listening to the cabin settle. He heard a chair creak. A cabinet door. Then nothing.

He took a breath and walked back down to the dock.

* * *

The dock was quieter at night.

The channel still carried sound—music drifting, an engine throttling up and down somewhere beyond the point—but it came thinner to their cove. The water moved in small strokes under the boards. The floats knocked once, then stopped.

Scott sat on the edge with his feet hanging over. His shoes were still on. He could smell dirt on his hands even after he'd washed them, the day stuck under his nails.

Behind him, the cabin lights glowed through the screen. His mother moved inside, shadow passing the window, the faint clink of a plate set down. His father's voice rose once, then fell again into a mumble.

Brian came down the steps without speaking. He stopped near the cleat and put his hand on the rope like he was checking it, the habit still there.

Matt followed a minute later and sat farther back on the boards, legs stretched out, beer in his hand. He didn't drink it right away.

For a while, none of them talked.

Scott watched the black shape of the channel between trees. He could picture the cliffs on the other side without wanting to. He could picture the ledge. The empty second.

Brian said, finally, "He's getting worse."

No one asked who.

Scott said, "Yeah."

Matt took a drink then, quick, like he needed his mouth busy. He wiped his thumb over the bottle label and looked down at the boards.

Brian kept his eyes on the water. "I don't know what we're supposed to do," he said.

The sentence surprised Scott. It came out small, almost like a mistake.

The ache rose in him. He wanted to say something that would help. He wanted it to land clean.

He said, "We've been doing it already."

Brian turned his head slightly, listening.

Scott stared down at his own shoes. "We just do the next thing," he said.

Matt snorted once, not amused. "That's your answer for everything," he said, but there wasn't heat in it.

Scott didn't argue. He looked past them toward the porch light and saw his mother step out onto the porch with a dish towel in her hand, hands already clean, needing something to do.

She didn't come down to them. She didn't call them in.

She stood there and watched the waterline for a moment, then went back in.

Brian said, quiet, "You saw him with that phone."

Scott didn't ask who. He knew.

Matt's jaw worked once. "I thought it was nothing," he said.

Brian said, "It wasn't nothing."

Silence sat between them again.

Scott looked at Brian's hand on the rope. The knuckles were white where he held it too tight.

Scott said, "We always do that."

Brian didn't move. "Do what?"

Scott felt the weight of speaking settle on him. He chose the smallest sentence he could.

"Decide what gets kept," he said.

Matt's head dipped as if he'd been hit.

Brian stared at the water, still holding the rope. When he spoke, his voice was even. "Sometimes you have to."

Scott nodded once, because it was true and because it wasn't the whole truth.

He didn't say the other part.

He let the words sit where they were.

* * *

Later, when Brian went back up to the cabin, Jake's phone lit up on the table.

Scott was in the kitchen rinsing a cup. Water ran over his hands, warm, then cooled as the heater caught up.

Jake's phone buzzed again. A name flashed on the screen.

TYLER

Scott reached out and turned the phone face down. The screen went dark.

From the living room, he heard Brian say something low to his son, not a lecture, not a question. Jake answered with one word and then nothing.

Scott dried his hands on the dish towel and walked past the table without looking at the phone again.

Outside, the dock knocked softly under the window, the lake settling into dark.

CH 30

The Straightened Road

TUESDAY NIGHT, after the inspector had gone and the yard had been tamped back down, Linda lit a small fire by the seawall.

It wasn't a bonfire the way it used to be when they were kids—no stacked pallets, no tall flame. Just a ring of limestone and a few split pieces of oak that caught slowly and then held.

Scott stood on the gravel with his hands in his pockets and watched the first smoke rise, thin and gray, drifting out over the cove.

The kids hovered close. Jake held a stick like he knew what to do with it. Emily pretended she didn't care, leaning against the seawall with her arms folded, but she kept her face turned toward the warmth. Owen sat on an overturned bucket and scrolled on his phone until Linda said, "Put it away."

Owen looked up. "Why?"

Linda didn't hesitate. "Because it's a fire," she said, and the reason was simple enough to be true.

Owen sighed, but he slid the phone into his pocket and watched the flame instead.

Brian came down from the cabin carrying a bag of marshmallows. He set it on the seawall like it was an offering. Jake grabbed one without asking.

Scott watched Brian's face in the firelight. The lines around his mouth were deeper than Scott remembered from the last time they'd all been together. Brian kept his shoulders squared as if holding himself in place took effort.

Matt arrived last, beer in his hand, sunglasses still on even though it was dark enough to be stupid. He sat on the seawall and stretched his legs out, toes in the gravel.

"This is nice," Matt said, too loud.

No one answered.

The fire cracked once. A spark rose and died.

Rick came down slowly, careful on the rocks. He carried nothing. Hat on. Hands empty. He sat on the low log they'd dragged over and leaned forward as if warming his palms, though his palms stayed open and still.

Scott felt the ache settle in him at the sight of his father there. Present and not fully present.

Linda sat beside Rick, close enough that her shoulder touched his. She didn't look at him when she did it. She looked at the fire, eyes narrowed, watching it like it might change.

Jake held his marshmallow too close and it caught. He yelped and shook the stick, flame licking up. Brian reached out fast and smothered it with his hand, bare palm, quick and practiced.

Jake stared at his father's hand. "Does that hurt?"

Brian flexed his fingers once. "A little," he said.

Jake watched him like he was waiting for a lesson.

Brian didn't give one.

Emily said, "You always do that," and Scott couldn't tell if she meant the fire or the saving.

Brian looked at her, then looked away. "Yeah," he said.

The channel carried a distant engine note, high and clean, and then it faded. The lake didn't look dangerous in the dark. It looked smooth. It always did.

Scott watched Owen watch the flame. Owen's face was lit and then not, lit and then not, as the fire shifted. For the first time that week, Owen looked like a kid.

Matt took a drink and said, "So what's the plan?"

Brian's head snapped toward him. "For what," he asked.

Matt shrugged. "For next year," he said, and Scott heard the trap in it. "For the cabin. For Dad."

Linda's shoulders went rigid.

Rick stared into the fire as if he hadn't heard his own name.

Scott felt the night narrow around them.

Brian said, "We get through tomorrow," and Scott heard the same sentence they'd said in the kitchen. First it had been Tuesday. Now it was just tomorrow. Always the next thing.

Matt's mouth pressed flat. "And then," he said.

Linda spoke before Scott could. "Then you go home," she said. Her voice was steady. "Then I stay."

Matt stared at her. "You can't do all this alone," he said.

Linda looked at him. In the firelight, her face looked older. Not fragile. Worn smooth by repetition.

"I have been," she said.

Silence held.

The kids kept roasting marshmallows, sensing the adult shift and not knowing where to put themselves. Emily leaned closer to Owen without thinking. Jake backed away from the fire a step and watched Brian's hand again.

Rick lifted his face toward the dark lake. "We drove down in the Corvette," he said suddenly, and Scott's chest tightened. "Remember that?"

Brian's eyes flicked toward Scott, quick. Matt laughed once under his breath like he was surprised to hear it said out loud.

Linda didn't correct Rick. She didn't tell him it was a different year. She let the memory exist.

Rick stared at the fire. "Three boys in the back," he said. "No seat belts."

Scott felt the words hit like a small stone.

Brian said, carefully, "Yeah," as if encouraging Rick to keep going might keep him anchored.

Rick nodded, satisfied. He said, "Your mom said stop at Foristell," and the name came out clear.

Scott looked at Linda.

Linda's face didn't change. But her eyes went wet in the firelight and then dried again as she blinked.

Matt said, "We were dying back there," and for a second his voice sounded like a boy's.

Rick smiled faintly. "You complained," he said.

"We always complain," Matt said.

Rick's smile faded as quickly as it had arrived. He looked down at his empty hands, then up again like he'd lost something.

Scott watched him and felt the ache of wanting the night to stay simple.

The fire popped and settled. Smoke rolled low for a second and then lifted.

Jake broke a marshmallow in half and handed a piece to Owen without being asked. Owen took it, surprised, and ate it without comment.

Emily watched them and then looked at Scott. "Were you like this," she asked, meaning all of it—the lake, the rules, the waiting.

Scott swallowed. "Yeah," he said. "We were."

Emily nodded like she could imagine it and like she couldn't.

Linda stood up first. She brushed ash from her jeans and said, "It's late."

The kids groaned, automatically.

Linda didn't argue. She just waited, and the waiting won.

Scott helped Rick up from the log. Rick's hand was light on Scott's arm, not the other way around.

They walked back toward the cabin, the fire behind them still burning, still holding.

Scott didn't know if the night had helped anything.

He only knew it had happened, which felt like a kind of proof.

* * *

The family left the cabin on Wednesday.

Not because everything was fixed. Because Tuesday had come and gone and the inspector had driven away. Brian had a long road back to North Carolina. Matt's watch kept shifting time zones when he looked at it. Julie had already been on the phone twice, lining up what happened after.

In the morning, the cabin filled with packing sounds—zippers, drawers, the scrape of a suitcase wheel over a threshold that caught.

Scott stood in the kitchen with a mug of coffee that had gone lukewarm and watched the room shift back toward departure.

His mother moved around the table with the same quiet purpose she'd had all those days, folding towels, stacking plates, putting things back where they belonged. She didn't say thank you. She didn't say don't go. She kept her hands busy.

His father sat at the end of the table with his hat on, keys in his palm. He turned the key ring slowly, metal clicking soft against metal.

"We going the back way?" his father asked.

Scott looked up. "Which back way?"

His father nodded toward the window as if the road was visible through the trees. "Past the store," he said. "You know. Down by the —"

The word didn't come.

He cleared his throat and lifted the keys a little. "The place with the bait."

"Alhonna," Scott said.

His father's face brightened with relief. "Yeah," he said. "That's it."

Scott waited for himself to correct something else—time, route, who drove last, where they were headed. He felt the old impulse rise and then he let it pass.

"We can," he said.

His father nodded, satisfied, and looked down at the keys again as if that had been the decision that mattered.

Brian came in carrying a cooler. He set it down too hard and then eased his hand off it, as if noticing his own force.

Julie stood by the counter with her phone in her hand, screen bright, thumb moving. Jake hovered near her, backpack already on. Emily leaned against the table with a sweatshirt tied around her waist, hair still damp from the dock.

Julie looked up at Brian. "We can't miss another day," she said, not accusing, just counting. Then her eyes dropped back to the screen and her thumb started moving again.

Matt came in last, sunglasses already on, car keys clipped to his belt like a tool.

"Let's go," he said, too cheerful.

No one answered.

* * *

Outside, the air was already warm.

The dock sat quiet in the cove, boards sun-bleached, rope tied, the waterline still lower than it should have been. The wave runners on the channel made their clean whining passes, sound rising and falling like it had nothing to do with the cabin.

Scott loaded the last bag into the back of his car and shut the hatch gently, as if sound could change what had happened.

His mother stood on the porch with her hands on her hips, not angry, just holding the shape of the goodbye. His father stood beside her, hat brim shading his eyes.

Brian hugged their mother quickly, one arm, hard. He nodded at their father and then stepped back as if he didn't know what else to do with his hands.

Matt hugged their mother longer, then patted their father on the shoulder as if they were friends.

Julie hugged Scott's mother too, quick and tight, like she was trying not to start anything she couldn't finish. Jake muttered goodbye without looking up. Emily said it clearly, like she meant it.

Two cabins down, Tyler's mother stood on her porch in the shade and watched them load the cars. She lifted one hand once, small.

His father smiled at the touch and then looked past them toward the water.

Scott stepped up last.

His mother touched his arm once. "Text me when you get home," she said.

He nodded. "I will."

His father leaned in, then stopped, unsure. "Drive safe," he said.

Scott said, "I will."

Behind him, Julie's car pulled out first, Jake's face in the window, Emily already looking at her phone. Brian's truck followed, taillights flashing once at the turn. Matt's rental idled a moment longer, then eased forward, Owen's silhouette still in the passenger seat.

Scott got into his car and shut the door. The sound was soft, final.

He pulled out of the gravel and onto the road, wider than it used to be. New gravel shoulders. Fresh paint. Guardrail in the places where there hadn't been anything but air.

Behind him, the cabin disappeared.

Before he reached the main road, he heard it one more time—the deep, sustained roar of a powerboat opening up somewhere on the channel, the sound rising and holding and then thinning as distance took it.

He didn't slow down to listen.

The road rose, then straightened.

Scott's hands stayed steady on the wheel. His body still waited for the old curve—the tight turn along the bluff where you had to commit before you could see what was coming.

But the county had cut it back. Shaved rock. A long, straight parkway you could take without thinking.

His heart tightened anyway.

When the view opened, it opened behind guardrail and new signs, the lake flat below him, bright in the morning, nothing like memory and exactly like it.

Scott didn't answer.

His father's voice came into his head without permission. Fast car. Windows down. Don't look at the view. Watch the road.

For a second he could smell hot brakes and hear the AM radio low under someone's talking.

Then it was gone.

He let the car keep moving.

About the Author

Warren Moss writes fiction about Mid-American families—brothers and parents, ordinary competence, and the long afterlife of what was never said. His work leans on physical detail and restrained interiority: docks that tap in the dark, roads that change, hands that keep checking ropes and knots. In his stories, faith is lived rather than performed, and danger arrives the way it often does in real life—casual, uncommented upon, with consequences that surface later.

The Straightened Road explores how memory moves through generations, and how responsibility can become both a form of love and a form of control. Three brothers return to a lake cabin on the Ozarks, where a father's fading memory and a long-buried summer force them to reckon with what they kept and what they let go.

The Straightened Road is his debut novel.

www.ingramcontent.com/pod-product-compliance
Lightning Source LLC
LaVergne TN
LVHW041917070526
838199LV00051BA/2654